God is inexperienced

Attempting his first novel, Chris almost accidentally creates a seedy couple and their backward son, living in Shepherd's Bush.

Although Chris can at first manipulate him, the man Ed soon outstrips his creator's intentions and control, and confronted with a choice between violence and mediocrity, chooses violence.

Ed has his own creation to play with. Although moronic, his son Tony is musically gifted, and the child's earnestness is a quality that proves irresistible to Ed's destructive, terrifying purpose.

This parable, at once powerful and pathetically haunting, forms a capsule of evil within the other novel: that of Chris's callow strivings as an author in search of a publisher – a wry, light-hearted contrast to his own taut, brilliant creation.

By the same author

Novels
The Bedsitter
Frame for Julian
A Year in Time
The Family
Martha on Sunday

Non-fiction
Actress

God is inexperienced

a novel by
Yvonne Mitchell

Constable London

First published in Great Britain 1974
by Constable and Company Ltd
10 Orange Street London WC2H 7EG
Copyright © 1974 Yvonne Mitchell
All rights reserved

ISBN 0 09 460430 4

Set in Intertype Plantin
Printed in Great Britain by
The Anchor Press Ltd
and bound by Wm Brendon & Son Ltd
both of Tiptree, Essex

To Cordelia

'Yes, I'm qualified.'

'Qualified!' said his father. 'What for, I should like to know?'

'For the dole.'

'Don't talk like that ...'

'I mean it, I now qualify for National Assistance. I've done six weeks' work, that's all you need ...'

'Where did you learn that trick?'

'Donald.'

'Donald's not on the dole. Donald's in electronics.'

'What do you understand by those words "in electronics"?'

'I don't want you to catechise me on my understanding,' said his father, 'Donald's in electronics.'

'Yes, but what do you *mean* by that?'

'By that I mean that he *works*, has to work pretty hard I should say, to get a modern scientific job like that.'

'Modern scientific my arse, sorry, Mother' – she was at a loss listening on the sidelines – 'he's in a *factory*.'

'Well?'

'In a *factory*, standing or possibly sitting by a machine that's spewing out parts. Donald's contribution to electronics, to modern scientific know-how, is to spot any defect in the spewed-out *parts*.'

He shouted the last word, hoped it sounded rude, and, to make sure his father recognised that it was, added 'Sorry, Mother,' again.

'At least he's working,' his father countered.

'So was I.'

'So *were* you.'

7

'I can earn more now by not working until I have to do another six weeks.'

'I can't stand it. . . . I can't stand this sort of attitude – it's not like you, Chris.' She had risen, tearful. 'You're not *really* like that.'

'I *am really* like that.'

'But you've never wanted money,' she said, 'never understood it, the wanting of money – you've even been foolish . . . not understanding that one *must* have . . .'

'He's been content to live on *my* money,' said his father.

'And now I can live on the State instead.'

'But you said only about . . . a few weeks ago, that you wanted to be a journalist . . .' she said, as if they had thought it a splendid idea.

'And what a reception *that* admission got.'

'How did you ever expect to do that sort of thing, we're not in that world.'

He could see that his father was trying to balance the horrors of journalism with those of living on the State.

'Who is, before they go into it?' he asked.

'People whose fathers before them . . . you can't just . . .'

'I know I can't.'

He hadn't even known to whom he should write. He had no qualifications. He had reported a few local incidents and sent them with a brief covering letter, suggesting working for them, to *The North London Weekly* – and he had a roneo'd reply. He imagined hundreds of men and women living in North London all writing the same letters with the same enclosures as himself and having the same replies. Better roneo the application next time. But there won't be a next time. I'm going to live on National Assistance in my father's house, and with my money I'm going to eat out and buy myself a huge and superb dictionary; reams of paper, carbon . . . and after the next six-week work-stint and subsequent dole . . . a typewriter; and I shall write. For myself, by myself. *What* I shall write I shall find out between now and buying the typewriter, so that once I put my finger on the thing . . .

'You're all the same . . .'

'You've just said Donald isn't.'

'Don't quibble words with me.'

'I'm not quibbling words, I'm quibbling meanings,' he said, 'attitudes, points of view, you can't think opposite things at the same time.'

'You know what your father means,' she said mildly.

Strange, that. I do know what he means, I know in spite of the fact that semantically he has no means of expression, I know despite the fact that what he means by any and everything is the opposite to what I mean and intend to mean by it. I understand the old bastard, simply by being in the same house as him all my life . . . that is, all the weekends and all the evenings of my life.

He regarded his mother for assessment. I don't know her, he admitted, except as a mother; because women function differently from us. I know what her reactions will be – but not why. I shall have difficulty writing women in my book, but it's about a woman I want to write, he decided suddenly. A *young* woman; the sort of young woman who . . .

The only woman he had known had not been young. Had in fact been the wife of a colleague, if that was the word, of his father's. The man had been in hospital and he had been told to see her home on the bus after she had dined with them. 'Been to supper', as she called it, and as his parents called it. Why was he such a semantic snob? he wondered. Her heavy carnation scent had invaded him on the double seat, her hips through the coat pressed against his. He would always like her because without her his introduction might not even now have taken place. How did one ever begin without a stroke of luck? Did one send a note, 'I have no qualifications, but I apply for entry; Yours sincerely'? And would they send roneo'd replies, all those lipsticked, hairdo'd, middle-aged, lower middle-

9

class women – like his mother? He couldn't imagine sleeping with her. She was too thin – too small – she lacked amplitude. Had his father found her satisfactory? He supposed so; or his father was perhaps unsatisfactory himself. He looked it. Desiccated at not yet fifty. Mild-eyed, sharp-tongued, neat as the figures he worked at . . . did they still use ledgers in Colliers? Or was his father now 'in automation', caught up in a machine, no longer asked to add and subtract?

But automation being in the unreliable state it was, he supposed his father was still being employed to check the machines' arithmetic, and would have the secret and supreme pleasure of finding it wrong. He would treat it no doubt as he had treated his son during those early years of homework – correcting his mistakes, showing how stupidly he had gone wrong on something so very simple; the compressed smile of knowing better tipping the corners of his mouth. Even then he had understood acutely the pleasure his father got in 'putting other people right'.

He had been made to see, early, not only at home but at school, and not only among the masters but among the boys too, that words were pretentious things and language an obsolete obscenity unless used to express everyday actions, or swear, or make appointments or point out faults; that the rightness and exactness of figures were the only things that made sense; the reality by which people lived, earned their living, communicated, got their pleasure, and got to the moon, and without understanding of them one was not only a nitwit, but a pretentious one who juggled with high-sounding words in order to try and impress.

The only other subject that had ever interested him was Nature Study and this had ceased to be in the curriculum once he left primary school. In those early years he had been happy learning about rocks, the stars, the creatures under the sea, from an enchanting creature called Miss Lilith. Miss Lilith was a beautiful study in herself, ash-blonde and gentle-voiced, and the class was always hushed when she talked of the mysteries of the world around them. The disenchantment with school and teachers after that early promise had made him recalcitrant, difficult to teach, dissatisfied. When he later found for himself the beauty of words, he realised there was no one to communicate with who was not likely to mock. He became a mocker himself, in self-defence.

'I'm going out.'

'At this hour?'

He went to his room and fetched the two small notebooks and a couple of biros and put them in his mac pocket. It was ten to eleven he saw by the sitting-room clock as he passed the door he had left open.

His mother repeated mildly as he passed, 'At this hour?' but he ignored it, and opened the front door.

An empty bus came after only seven minutes. He sat alone, up behind the driver's back.

'All the way,' he said to the conductress.

'At this hour?' she said, as if it were a great joke. She had a filthy cold, her fingers were bluish and chapped, and there was a thick dark line surrounding her parting where the peroxide had grown out.

Nevertheless he asked her, 'D'you go off duty then?'

His tone was obvious.

'Get along with you,' she said. 'I've got a husband.'

'So?'

'Get along with you,' she said again. She sat just behind him and started humming.

He took no notice. If she wasn't going to oblige he had no use for her, silly cow. He wanted to concentrate on the book.

'Got a job?' she asked, looking at his face in the driver's dark-coated back.

'Shut up,' he said. 'I'm trying to work.'

'Looks like it.' She got up and sauntered to the back of her bus, humming louder, to annoy him.

A West Indian got on at the next stop. She held him in conversation, again to annoy . . . the weather, job, ah well, that's life for you, that's what I always say, got to take the rough with the smooth, clearing up a bit, forecast says rain, this country, standing all day, could do with a nice cup of tea *ad nauseam ad vomitum* – why didn't they talk in figures, what the hell good were words to them.

'Hendon Central,' she called as if whole crowds wanted to know where they were . . . go along here dear and take the first, no let me see, the second to the right and you can't miss it, it's on the corner, if it's not the first right it's the second or third you can't miss it, I said what a thing to say I said; talking to me like that don't you talk to me like that I said or I'll give you a piece of my mind I said I never heard of such a thing at your age I don't know what we're coming to I said I said I said I said. I said nothing – ever – that said anything, Platt's Lane, I said.

It would be about a girl – not too pretty but young, sexy . . . who are her parents, what sort of background?

He got out one of the notebooks and a biro and wrote GIRL. SEXY. He began to doodle, trying to imagine a face or a father, a place or a time. He made a list. Place? Time? Father?

He had decided by the time the bus stopped under Selfridges' clock that the girl lived near Piccadilly Circus. Soho perhaps. He could walk there tonight and make notes about it – the names of streets, shops, the sort of people, taxis passing. He wrote the word 'Taxi' – it might help. He was busy doodling, trying to fix on the colour of her hair as a clue to her, when the bus stopped and he saw the driver getting down backwards, cramp-legged from his booth. He got up. The conductress was already on the pavement, going to have a word with the driver, he supposed. What word? It wouldn't signify whatever it was. 'Night' . . . 'Raining' . . . 'Cheerio' . . . There were many to choose from that would not commit her. Stupid cow, he said to her, but far enough away for her not to hear.

He had an irrational jealousy of her. She had a mate to work with, a husband to go home to, and a job. She made contact with her customers, passed the time of day or night with them, she could hum, peroxide her hair, knit herself mittens – she had a whole enviable fulfilled life, whilst he . . . silly cow, he said again, and wished violently that she would get rid of her husband for one hour and take him to her bed. He put the notebook and biro in his pocket, walked quickly down Regent Street without noticing it, and turned left into Shaftesbury Avenue.

A café was open. Exactly the kind of place he had hoped for . . . Golden Egg – Wimpy – espresso type; small, nearly empty, music, tables good for writing on; the sort of place where one could order coffee and sit without further request or interruption for hours. He would save wandering around Soho until he had had a warming coffee and made some more notes and thought about the colour of the girl's hair. Maybe in Soho he would meet a girl or a woman who . . . not one who would do for the book, no, he wanted to think that one up, but one who would do for the night. For half an hour even; ten minutes. . . .

He ordered the coffee from a man behind the machine, and thought of Iris, who had sat pushing her thigh against his on the bus ride home, and had later taken off her suspender belt for him, and rolled down her stockings, and told him how she missed her husband in hospital. He had come out of hospital within the week, the lucky bastard, and would be having her now; her lovely uneven flesh with its dimpled buttocks and goose-pimpled thighs. Lucky bastard. He had been successful at once, surprised, delighted and immensely proud, but she had sent him downstairs to make coffee, angry with him, irritated. 'You may have satisfied yourself but what about me' and only an hour later she had made him understand and he had satisfied them both. I am part of the human race he had told himself, I fuck, therefore I am.

But he needed her again badly, and if not her then another; any. Meanwhile the girl with the blonde hair question-mark eluded him. What did he know of girls? Nothing. He would have to invent her without help from any model. To his heart's desire. She is in love, he decided at once; she is standing in Piccadilly Circus, her fingers entwined with . . . his first vision of her lover was of himself, but he forced himself to substitute a dark, broad-shouldered type who didn't suit her. Why had she chosen him for God's sake? Silly bitch. Eros was poised, ridiculously unerotic, on his pedestal above them. They sat on the steps, there was just room between a dirty girl hanging her head in lonely drugged unhappiness, and a bearded boy, lightly strumming his guitar for whom whatever he had taken had taken; and had taken him to his own underworld of happiness. But the girl, Chris's own girl (yes, she had long fair hair he decided) was not addicted, she said, to anything. 'Tried once – don't know what it was, snow I think someone said, but it didn't do anything for me.'

'I've never tried,' he confessed. The young man still insisted on looking like himself, though he tried hard to see him dark and squat. If I give him a name and put pimples on him? No, she wouldn't like pimples. A name, and a limp perhaps – she might be partial to a bit of a limp, left over after a childish polio – paralysed for a year aged five, irrelevant now but might come in handy later – yes a limp it is, that will distinguish him from me. 'Dark', he wrote, 'limps', and bit his thumbnail for a name. The coffee was cold now. He ordered another, felt happy, full of achievement. When I've drunk it I'll walk around Soho, make a note of street names, and find a woman. He grew impatient waiting for the coffee. The café clock hands pointed to one o'clock. He pocketed his notes and the biro, put four square lumps of sugar in the coffee, drank and paid. Perhaps I should try heroin – marijuana – whatever, I don't know which are the safe ones. Pot. Of course. Nonsense about police raids. Father has a medicine chest full of

14

chemist stuff which he doesn't recognise as drugs. Drugs, you idiot father, the lot of them – I'd love the police to search and carry you off, protesting – Frith Street, Old Compton, Dean – a fat old girl smiled at him. 'Try second alley on the left, duckie,' she said. Did they really talk like that! 'Green door – first floor.' She smiled again and hugged her too short coat to her, crossing her arms for warmth, and coughed resoundingly.

He found the green door and pushed it. It opened on to a straight steep staircase. A girl was coming down sideways, her knee bleeding slightly, her stocking torn. She stopped and dabbed it with a licked finger. 'She won't be long,' she said to him, but without glancing at him, 'had to go out for a bit. Wait upstairs if you like.' She passed him and went into the street. He stood for a moment and then followed her.

The fat old girl was still at the corner. 'Nothing doing,' he told her.

'Nothing doing?' She looked surprised. 'Oh I *am* sorry, dear.'

'Have you got anywhere?'

'I've got an awful cough.'

'I don't catch things easily.'

'I haven't got anything else.'

'No,' he felt himself blush, 'I didn't mean anything – by it . . . nothing.'

She waddled away from him.

He followed, hating himself for his insensitive remark.

She led him back to the same green door. 'Wonder where she's gone then,' she said to herself as she puffed up the stairs. She turned the cardboard hanging on the door which said 'gone out' to the other side on which was written 'occupied', and led him in.

It appeared to be a photographer's studio – there were luscious, lewd photographs of women and parts of women. She said 'Come on then,' and took him behind a curtain. A

15

changing-room, he supposed. There was a table with spilled powder on it, and a cracked mirror. . . .

'When he left' – he imagined the printed words on the page, and said them aloud, laughing . . . 'when he left . . .' I won't write like that – if ever I get inside my girl I shall write from the inside. 'If you see what I mean,' he said again aloud, and laughed. The fat old girl had made him happy, released him, perhaps too she had released some other sort of creativity in him. He would see.

He walked to Piccadilly Circus, to the meeting place, to the fair girl with the long hair. Perhaps now he would find her there. Unlikely at this hour, he thought, as he got nearer, finding himself suddenly inexplicably shy. And unlikely that she'd be alone if she looked as he wanted her to, so there was no need for this holding back, this fear that she might indeed appear to him.

There were still a few taxis and cars; rain began to spot the pavement. Boots was open, a small queue he could discern still at the drug counter. There were a few people on the steps of Eros; none of them his girl; none of them resembling any of the ones he had thought up. 'Except myself,' he said, twisting his lips with the pleasurable irony of it, and recognising the trick of his father's mouth, 'except myself, except myself, and I don't want him to look like that anyway, and anyway I haven't got a limp.' Nevertheless he limped, or hopped, up a couple of steps, and put his mac down to sit on, extracting first the notebook and biro. What a yawning bore, he thought, as he tried to write a word, any word; what a bore. He was cold, uninterested in anything. I've written myself out for the day, he consoled himself, and at least I know who I'm looking for. Something will come of it. A clock struck three. If I walk home I should be in before six, even with a few stops on the way. She'll think I've left home . . . 'old enough to look after himself, you can't mother him all his life'. . . . 'Yes, but he's never been out so late before.' 'Turn over and go to sleep.' He saw his mother's inexpressive blue eyes wide open, her body rigid with listening. 'Go to sleep, you silly cow,' he said for his father; and picking up his mac started to walk up Regent Street.

He resented the noises his father made in the house in the mornings. Seven-twenty exactly, that screeching alarm, then shuffle-pad-pad outside his door to the lavatory, the discreet shifting of phlegm in the throat as he passed, the Niagara flushing of the thing – he even gave in to an irrational belief that he did it over-loudly on purpose to wake him, to 'show' him, to reproach him (How on earth can Mother live with it; as I do – as I do – no choice); and between the metal clank of the bathroom door being shut and the satisfied clicking announcement of its opening (I've *done* my business, I'm a good boy I am) the revolting spreading stink of fatty bacon.

He stayed in bed till two in the afternoons. She no longer tapped on the door to ask if he was hungry, just left things around in the kitchen for when he came down. As if I'm ill – a case. That is of course how they think of me – he'll be discreetly enquiring at work about trick cyclists – the shame of having a son who stays in bed, doesn't work, pretends he's writing a book – a sure case for the analyst . . . and yet we've done our best.

He lay, thinking and not thinking – doodling and making single-word notes, the face of the girl still eluding him, the personality non-existent. He didn't even want sex with her because he had given her no body – but she was with him all the time, her shadowy fingers on his arm as the biro blotched, as he cut a hunk of bread, as he sugared his tea.

One day he woke to a remembered dream. He recalled it, re-piecing it, and for once the grating noises failed to impinge on his consciousness. There were twins. Twin girls; large buxom girls, long-legged, thick thighed, thick-lipped.

One was fair and one was dark. But there was another and more striking difference. The fair one had no head. 'What a pity,' clucked everyone, 'such a *pretty* girl, prettier than her sister, and oh dear isn't it dreadful, my dear, she has no head.' It wasn't an accident as far as he could discover, listening – she was born like it; born the prettier of the two, the fair one, without a head. He too felt desperately sorry when he heard about her; and an immense compassion when he actually saw her. It was true. She was alas a freak.

Thinking over the dream, his diaphragm laughing at the ingenuity of it, he could see its obvious symbolic meaning. 'I'm trying to create a girl who doesn't exist. Who can't exist, because she was born dead.'

The uncreated girl for once left him alone – or rather deserted him, and he sat in bed feeling empty and futile. The thought of a stint in a factory seemed attractive; perhaps after all what he was doing was in truth what his father and mother believed: wasting his time, opting out, lying about, pretending, cheating. I can't write – what on earth part of me ever suggested to myself that I could? The shirker, the real me, the pretender, the cheat. I am as they see me. He closed his eyes. The smell of bacon was still pungent in the small room. He could hear her hoovering the carpet downstairs. He got up, it was only ten o'clock, and surprised his mother in curlers, a duster in her hand, a goddam awful flowered pinny over her pink candlewick dressing-gown.

'What are you doing up?' she said, caught before she had time to arrange her thoughts and so choose her words. Yes, she had been thinking of me as an invalid.

'I'm going to take a day off.' He put the quarter-pound slab of butter on one slice of crumbling boiled over-white bread, while she watched him with pity and with cautious non-understanding.

'I'm so glad you're better dear.'

'It's a slow process,' he said seriously – after all there was no one else to talk to – she might be a good listener, he had never tried her out. But on second thoughts he knew that anything that he wanted to express had best be kept for his notebook, or it would never be entered there as a secondary receiver of ideas. Once spoken, a thought, an idea lost its potency and its charm. It had to be written to keep itself intact.

He left the kitchen, humming, and she went back to the living-room to resume her hoovering. He took the two notebooks and the biro from the bed, put them in his mac pocket, patted the pocket, saying 'Good dog' and went briskly out of the house. It was much colder than he had expected, and windy. He walked quickly, purposefully, towards the corner shop confectioner-tobacconist, which also sold pads of writing paper. He pointed to the shelf and held up two fingers.

'Two?' she said.

'Yah.' He wanted to sound young, impatient, a writer, which was after all what he was . . . nearly.

'Lined?' she asked.

'Lined?'

'Lined paper,' she said, and flicked the pages to show him.

'Nah,' he said, '. . . got a ruler, like to make my own.'

'Saves time to buy it already lined for you . . .' she suggested hopefully.

He simulated losing his temper. 'But that's what I *want* it for,' he said, thumping his fist on the counter. 'I've been given a ruler and I want to try it out! On unlined paper! I want to make my own lines,' he added feebly.

She was properly impressed. 'Sorry,' she muttered, you saw all sorts serving in a shop, chap came in today quite young too round the bend wanted to make his own lines, said his friend had given him a present of a ruler, I tell you you see life . . . if I could write I could tell them a thing or two; might do one day, you never know . . . when I'm retired perhaps (laughs, because that day is so distant) haven't the time now, I've been that busy. . . .

He was wandering round the Miró exhibition at the Hayward, he'd been here before for the Pop Art and had thought he himself could have done better – if he'd wanted to, which he certainly didn't. He recognised this attitude as that of his father towards anything that he, Chris, liked . . . (they would be exactly the feelings of his father towards this Miró stuff for instance) and wondered where he could put his finger on the certainty that he was right when he took the attitude, and his father wrong.

This painter Joan Miró's work was bubbling with excitement, and uncommitted, unrigid, youth. How had she first dared to make these childish marks in all seriousness? What had her parents said? 'A child could do better'? No, Miró hadn't come from North London, she'd probably come from somewhere in Italy – maybe her parents had just touched their foreheads with a finger and said 'gaga'. And what did the Miró ma and pa feel when their gaga (or whatever the Italian is for nuts) daughter got praise from professional painters and critics?

Did they assume then that all artists were gaga plus those who pretended to admire them, and cross themselves and be grateful that at least it had brought in the money? Not that he, Chris, had ever pretended to himself that he was going to be a highly successful and admired writer. . . . No, he felt he would always bask in an atmosphere of failure . . . it was just that he wanted to write, to use words on paper, to redeem them from the degradation of being kicked back inside him in his youth as something not only shameful, but out-of-date.

He stood absorbed in a painting that had gone back into the discovery of a time of childhood that Chris had almost forgotten. Slight twinges of sense-memory nearly caught him, and were gone again. There was a girl looking at the dancing shapes standing about two pictures away; a typical art student, coarse cloak, unwashed hair, bare legs; very young, earnest, proud. He smiled at her and she turned away, not brushing him off, but uncertain, vulnerable.

'Fabulous girl, isn't she?' he ventured.

There was a pause, he thought she wasn't going to answer, and then she said, 'Who?'

'Joan Miró.'

'He's an old man.'

'I know,' said Chris, dissolving in a pool of sweat. 'Fabulous old girl.'

She turned away, at least she wasn't sure. . . . When the fever died down and he suspected he might be normal, he tried again:

'There's a coffee room at the Festival Hall, come and have one?'

'Are you going to the concert?' Her voice was high and thin.

'Might do.'

She shrugged and moved away to look at a picture.

'What's wrong with going to a concert then?' he bluffed.

'Wouldn't get in.'

'Why not?'

'Don't be daft, it's Barenboim.'

She hadn't looked at him yet, was slowly looking at one, then a second picture, leaving long gaps between each of his questions and her answer. . . .

'Besides, I want to look.' He looked with her, careful not to give an opinion, sometimes choosing a different one from her to stand in front of . . . though his interest was waning. After a quarter of an hour she relented. . . . 'We might queue for returns.'

For an hour and a half they queued, outside, behind about twenty others, until the door opened and they became part of the official queue for returns, which was now of considerable length. This Barenboim was probably another fabulous old man – he wasn't going to stick his neck out again in case she turned out to be a fat old German soprano.

Of course, on reflection, how could he have thought a young woman would have had an exhibition at the Hayward Gallery all to herself? They were all old, the really successful ones; but he certainly wasn't going to grudge old man Miró his success. Why wasn't youth as light and as certain, instead of being such a drag? The queue inched forward; he wanted a coffee badly, but was wary of opening any conversation with a girl who knew that Joan was an old man's name, and no doubt knew also what Barenboim's first name was. He played with a few possibles: Walter, Franz, Enriques, or if it's a woman Elizabeth (I'll bet it's Elizabeth) Maria, Helga . . . the girl had taken out a piece of plasticine from her bag and was rubbing it between her fingers; a superstition? No questions; it would all be known soon, and he'd lie in bed at home having heard Barenboim and knowing that Joan was the name of an old man.

When they were at the front of the queue, a short eager man rushed passed them, and pushed two white pieces of paper under the bars of the box-office window. . . . Chris felt for his money and began to say, as he'd heard the man in front of him in the queue say, 'How much?' But the girl grabbed his clothing and pulled him aside.

'Expensive ones,' she whispered. She tugged him again almost at once, saying 'Yes' to a fat foreign-looking girl who was showing her some greyish tickets with a red line. 'Quick.' She was handing over some money herself then held out her hand for his – '5op, haven't you got any change . . . ?'

They ran up the wide first staircase; excitement gripped him, caught he supposed from other couples, hand in hand, leaping up three stairs at a time. Thronging, that's the word, he said to himself, we're a throng thronging.

Part of his elation was due to the fact that he'd caught sight of a poster with Daniel on it. Daniel Barenboim and Jacqueline Dupré; so may be these two played double pianos or he played and she sang. Anyway, he liked the name Dupré, she was bound to be French; or, the thought suddenly struck him, were French men sometimes called Jacqueline? The girl seemed certain of where the grey tickets should take them . . . up and up he raced with her; flurry, rush, scurry, anyone would think it was the last train out of somewhere or tickets for the Big Fight.

'I shall expect a good match after all this,' he said.

On the top floor she aimed at a far door. His first sight of the hall made him feel uncouth; and yet the people up here were dressed more or less as he was, looked no more 'classy'. Long-haired men in macs, almost indistinguishable from himself – bare-legged girls with no make-up, like the girl with him – no it wasn't they who made him feel out of place, it was the place itself . . . something to do with its spaciousness, an entirely different sensation from coming into a large cinema; whatever the reason it gave him agoraphobia . . . he didn't mind the height, he told himself as he followed her up the steep steps to their seats – looking behind him and down dizzily – it was the space. And yet it wasn't all that vast. He felt better when he sat down, proteced from the drop by a large bald man in the seat in front. He slid down until his legs were under the bald man's seat. 'Rather have my legs broken than fall to the bottom.' He looked at his watch – four minutes to go, and no chance of going down and up again in that time to get a coffee, even supposing he could face the descent.

The orchestra were there – distant, small. He wasn't going to see much of their faces from here, Barenboim's and Dupré's: he'd decided by now they were tenor and soprano as there was no sign of a piano . . . he didn't want to sit through an evening of singing – he was bound to giggle like a schoolgirl if they made those singing-into-jug noises that some of the singers he'd heard on the radio made . . . he was tempted to start a mock *lied* (he'd done that in front of a mirror before now, to his own delight) . . . or maybe old Daniel was one of those penguin conductors, stiff-backed, flapping his wings heavily up and down but never leaving the ground – his black tail feathers split low down the back – while Madame Dupré sang into a china jug; a tightly-corseted bulging little woman, still pretty, dumpily outstretching her dimpled short arms to the audience as she sang, her hair as tightly arranged as her body, reddish from the hairdresser's, pomaded so as not to move as her head tossed the top notes upwards. The audience will think her marvellous, and she will blow kisses to them while the penguin conductor bows, beams, and gently applauds her as well. Oh well, successful people had been young once, he supposed, might even not have been all that brilliant to begin with; they'd have to be trained, tour around for years before being spotted by some talent scout.

The scout, khaki shorts just above his knobbly knees, was inspecting the ranks of would-be successful singers, dancers and writers; stopping now and then to ask one of them to sing a note or do a pirouette, pinning a red spot on the shoulders of those he tipped for future success, an outburst of clapping and on to the stage came at a brisk pace a young man in impeccable modern gear – dark-haired – must be around twenty-four or . . . again before he had time to finish a thought the audience hushed, the man held up his arms and the music started.

It was its immediacy that held him – he didn't care that he didn't know what was being played (hadn't entered his head to find out if they had programmes at these things) he didn't even mind whether this was Herr B or Monsieur Jacqueline D – he was happy – as happy as he could remember. He picked up his legs and leaned forward; he had a girl at his side and music in his ears.

24

Wow! The overture was short. He joined in the applause unselfconsciously, for the first time in years not seeing himself behaving, but just getting on with the joyous business of reacting without pretending. There wasn't much of a pause before young Danny or Jackie (whichever he was) was back again, this time followed by a smashing girl with long fair hair, striding briskly in her long evening dress carrying a hockey-stick, no it wasn't it was a 'cello; she was going on to the sportsground with a 'cello, and he'd bet she'd score a goal with it too. She sat down, spread her skirt wide behind the 'cello, gave young Danny a loving grin and, tossing her mane like a spirited mare, broke into the first bars of whatever it was, the orchestra ridden by young Dan cheering her on, pacing her, out-racing her, then giving her her head; until they finally landed up neck and neck at the tape.

The extraordinary thing about the whole evening was that for the first time he could remember his envy juices weren't working. He had grown so used to living with them that he had never before now registered them as such. Now that they were released and drained from him he felt as if a huge pus-y boil that he had carried on his neck all his life had suddenly been opened and left him not only elated and appreciative, but able to allow himself to show that he was. All those rotten money-making film stars and pop singers, all those cheap and successful pornographers, all those 'top' people – the photographers and publicists – the thought of whom had built up so much gall in him, could now get on with their futile and putrid lives without bothering him – he was free to admire now. What surprised him most about himself was his wholehearted admiration of the *man*. He was intensely relieved to find that he *could* admire, if another man, however young, deserved it, and truthful enough to admit that he had no business to expect anything of himself until he had made up for a lost childhood and youth by working as hard as this Daniel boy must have. He can only be about eight or nine years older than I am . . . I vow that for the next eight years I'll...

Satiated with pleasure and sound, he and the girl made for the coffee-bar. Until now he had forgotten that that was why he'd asked her here. They queued for trays without speaking. . . . He took a coffee, a dried-up salad, a triangle of cheese in silver paper; two elderly slices of cake, a blancmangy-looking object in a square ridged carton, and two rolls. The girl said she didn't want to eat.

They sat stirring their coffees in silence.

'Live in London?' he asked – recollecting from his far-back meeting over three hours ago that she liked short sentences.

'In the week. You?'

'Yes.' There was a long pause and then he added, 'Week-ends too.'

He was pleased to be able to catch her rhythm – almost mimic her; he felt no cruelty in doing so, only a sort of get-togetherness. He could hardly expect her to catch *his* rhythm – whatever it was. He wondered if he had one, or was just a catcher of other people's.

She was silent, but she quite obviously wasn't a blank. Either she was remembering the music or making up her mind to say something.

'I share with four others,' she said at last to her coffee.

'Well, that's a lot of help,' he said; and added falsetto, 'I'm not very strong; two's the most I can manage.'

She watched him eat. Either she didn't understand him, or she understood him well.

'So, it's not fair to ask you to see me home.'

She spoke jerkily, suddenly, as if she were not only not used to saying much, but extremely unskilled in dealing with strangers.

'Where is it?'

'South Ken.'

'It's on my way!' he said triumphantly, wondering why he

was letting himself in for a long night's walk home. 'Do you all doss in the same room?'

She said, looking into her cup, as if seeing the answer there in a crystal ball, 'I'm with one, the other room's three.'

'What's her name?'

'Who? Kate?'

'Kate ever away?'

She didn't answer.

'Where are you weekends?'

'At home.'

'Where's home?'

'Eastbourne.'

He left the bargaining or mating, or whatever this conversational procedure could be called, at that.

He wasn't sure yet whether he liked her; sitting across the table from her he remembered the streakiness of her legs and feet, as if rivulets of rain had run down a dusty surface . . . anyway he'd see her home tonight . . . no need to pursue it further; South Ken was one hell of a way from Palmer's Green.

At the platform Claire showed her day-return ticket to Eastbourne, and he realised he hadn't bought his. He went to the queue at the ticket office pigeon-holes, where the protected men were scarcely visible in their cages. Not as good as the zoo, he thought. He put a piece of sugar on the turntable. The balding, spectacled, shirt-sleeved man ignored it and waited for the money.

'How much?'

'Two ten.'

'Day return?'

'You didn't say day,' said the badger or llama or whatever it was he was trying to feed; and angrily fetched another ticket, slipping the unwanted one under the bench in front of him. To show his irritation at being kept waiting while the young idiot fumbled in his mac pockets for money, he wiggled the wax in his left ear with his fourth finger, looked at the result and started wiggling again.

'Found anything interesting?'

Claire was waiting by the barrier.

'You were ages,' she said.

'Got held up by a dromedary.'

'A what?'

She never expected replies. She punctuated a lot of his sentences with 'what' – 'the what' – 'a what' – which meant in her vocabulary 'I heard what you said but it was silly.'

In the dusty carriage they added more dust by putting their feet up on the opposite seats until other people came and sat on the sole-marks. He noticed the soft newly-washed skin of her feet, and the childish cut toenails and wondered whether she'd done it for him, for her parents, or because she'd looked down one day and seen them.

She stuck her fingers between his, the rings she'd made herself pressing sharply into his flesh.

'You won't like them.'

'You wouldn't like mine.'

'I mean, they're so prim.' She was touchingly embarrassed; despising herself for old-fashioned intolerance, and yet wanting to forestall him, so that he'd go on thinking well of her. She reddened and looked out of the window.

'My father's done time,' he said, 'and my mother's a char.'

She looked at him.

'Honest?'

'No,' he said.

She took out a lump of plasticine and pulled a piece off for him.

'Want some?'

He pulled a face of fear at it, cartoon fear.

'Does it bite?'

She rolled the pulled-off piece back into the lump, and

28

moulded and pressed and warmed it with her fingers.

'What're you making?'

'I'm not.'

'What're you not making?'

'I'm exercising. Keeping my fingers supple.'

'Do you like that?'

'Love it.'

'I'm jealous,' he said moodily.

'I offered you some.'

He knew nothing of jealousy, couldn't even imagine it, though he had known envy like an illness. It was one of the few genuine feelings he had experienced – that and his hatred of the smirk on his father's and his own mouth. And yet his envy had never goaded him into ambition. It lacked energy. Was he, he wondered, ambitious or even energetic enough to write a book? And, awful thought, did he really *want* to write, or did he just want to be a writer? I shall begin, he decided, and find out afterwards which it is I want, otherwise I shall never know.

She leaned her head against his shoulder and he suddenly felt that life was a good thing, good enough to swallow up all his failings, that as long as she put her head on his shoulder and fiddled with that stuff, that he had a place somewhere, and a meaning.

'My father's got this awful smirk on his face like mine when I pretend to be clever,' he murmured into her hair. She understood. She said quietly back, 'They're anxious as if they're going to lose their job all day. My dad was born with tacks in his mouth.' That was one cliché he hadn't heard before. 'He lays carpets,' she said, 'and undercarpets, used to creeping about in carpet overshoes, and not being able to answer because of the tacks.'

'My mum's in hoovering,' he said, 'every day the same room.'

'Mine's in the post office.'

He was content; he'd be able to cope, not make a fool of himself; they'd be just like his own background – he needn't be afraid.

They took a twenty-minute bus ride after leaving the station, and then a ten-minute hill-climbing walk between row after row of large houses, all split into flats, she told him, except the boarding houses. The wind was harsh, penetrating.

'How do you manage without stockings?' he asked.

'Without *what*? . . .' she rebuked him contemptuously.

She pressed a second-floor button which said Prescott on it. He'd bet himself it would be the second floor because he'd seen the curtain move discreetly as they approached. Poor Claire, was she as nervous as he was?

'Keep your pecker up,' he whispered and kissed her earlobe. Keep your *what*?' he mimicked for her, 'pecker,' he said, 'P.E.K.K.A.' She gave him a shove and they were giggling as Mrs Prescott opened the door. He felt himself redden.

'Hallo,' said Mrs Prescott brightly, 'hallo, Claire dear, was the train a bit late?'

'Don't think so. Dad in?'

'Yes, he's upstairs.'

Chris stood aside to let her go up the stairs before him, terrified lest he should make it look like a gesture, bow, sweep his hand, something ghastly. They stumped without talking up to the second floor. Mr Prescott was sitting in front of the television; he half rose, nodded 'Glad to know you' and sat back again.

'Can't you even leave that thing to *kiss* me,' Claire said.

He took her hand, and patted it, and pulled her down to kiss him . . . 'It's racing,' he said, 'won't be long.'

He was many years older than his wife, who in fact looked still a girl, thinner than Claire, prettier, but prim. Tight shut. I'll have to play them as if they were grandparents, he decided. He was about to sit down near Mr Prescott when Mrs Prescott said 'Do you want to wash or anything?'

He longed to say 'wash or *what*?' but instead reddened and
said 'No thank you'. Mr Prescott's mouth was indeed moving
as if he'd got tacks in it. How people can go to bed with people
who've got habits . . . he put his hand up to cover his mouth
as he found himself unconsciously sucking imaginary tacks.

On the table was a lacy cloth, and a dainty tea-service; little
pearl-handled forks; he realised that he was the reason for all
this wedding-gift refinement; it was all there to appease him.
His impulse was to get up and run for his life back to the
station, but he visualised his mother doing the identical thing
should he ever – God forbid – ask Claire home, and knew
with a deep pang how lost he would be if she should get up
and run from him because of the panic induced by lacy
tablecloths and dainty forks. He held himself down in his chair
by grasping the undersides of it tightly, and then released them
as he realised it looked as if he needed the lavatory suddenly
and urgently; and tried to concentrate on the television.

'Just going to make the tea,' Mrs Prescott said, and almost
backed out of the room. He took the opportunity to comb his
hair. Long thin individual hairs came out in the small comb,
which he hastily stuffed back in his pocket. Why did he feel it
necessary to play the same game? To appease their appease-
ment? Was it love for Claire, or cowardice, a lack of conviction, or an acceptance that this was what he'd have to accept
as life. Not with Claire, he decided, looking at her thighs
which were thawing from the purple the wind had blown into
them, and were very nearly pretty. She's too coarse, she'll
never fall into the dainty . . . nevertheless he wasn't convinced
that he wanted coarseness nor her special brand of artiness to
be part of his future . . . why did he think it would have to?
They were neither of them committed to spending the rest of
their lives together . . . months would do – even a year if
nothing changed either of them. He relaxed back in his chair
and crossed his arms, then his legs. I'm behaving well, he told
himself, and as he was used to behaving rather than being,

he accepted that that was all he could expect of himself.

She was still sitting under Eros, bare-legged – no, he decided, looking without desire at those other bare legs, no, she is trousered; she wears a pair of . . . they were talking, she and her dark boy-friend, interminably talking, her arms had drawn up her long trousered legs, so that her chin could rest reflectively on her knees. . . . She didn't look at her companion, nor he at her; but it was clear that they were absorbed in each other. Chris climbed the steps at the back of them and tried to hear what they were saying, but they were keeping it private, mumbling. 'Don't just sit there,' he said to them, 'get moving' – 'get along there please.' 'Get UP for God's sake, don't just sit there talking – and with your backs to me all the time.' Every time he walked round the other side of them to have a look at their faces, they turned away and presented their backs again to him. Nevertheless, patient as a bird-watcher, notebook in hand, he circled and recircled the statue to get his data.

'. . . A piece of cake . . .'

He forced himself to rejoin Claire's mother and the dainty flowered tea-pot. In that moment of return, between unconsciously putting out his hand for the proffered cake, and placing his fingers on its jammy side, he had time not only for an expectation of boredom as he relinquished the steps of Eros, but a large film sequence in which he and his parents re-enacted scenes from his daily life in the claustrophobia of the 'room' at home, and, as the jam seeped on to his finger and thumb, the film was overlaid by physical panic and the knowledge that this – that – them – cake, tea-pot, hoover, was a trap that was strangling the life out of him. Rudely, abruptly, his voice constricted but with enough left in him of that natural acting ability which helped him whenever he wished to cheat, looking at his watch, he heard his voice as if it were placed inside his ears, saying that he had to take an earlier train than Claire.

The pained surprise on her face, which he had, of course, expected, irritated him – 'I *told* you I'd have to leave early . . . because of . . . really your memory!' He said the last word gaily, heard the laughter in his head; smiling compassionately at her, at female inability to recollect what people *said*.

The hill, the biting wind, the cold station, the hot compartment, telescoped into a concentrated effort to keep still the trembling of his knees and subdue the pounding in his ears. He clung on to his illness as obstinately as a child who will only vomit in the known lavatory; hugging it for an eternity of three hours and twenty minutes; fixing in his mind a tiny lit Piccadilly Circus at the end of the hellish tunnel.

His head splitting, his limbs weighted, conscious that all the time he had been heading for just this, he reached his home; though why he should rush with such desperate need towards the thing he wished to avoid, only his illness could tell him.

It was evening. He surprised his mother in a wispy dressing-gown, her thin hair wound round pretty pink slug-like curlers, standing outside his room. She looked guilty; said as if she'd spoken to him only five minutes ago:

'Can I go into your room, dear?'

'You can hoover all night if you like,' he said weakly, his sickness receding.

'No, I hoovered this morning,' she answered seriously, 'I'd just like to make sure everything's tidy.'

He kissed her on the forehead, but on his way to the lavatory he added 'Enjoy yourself'. Why did he always betray with such remarks his real self, the self with the curved and secret meanness in the lip which was his father's. Why did one side of him despise the petty, the mean and the insensitive, whilst the actual, living, daily side performed petty mean and insensitive actions? Why did he hold such admiration for the exact word, for the beauty of semantics, when his true self quite obviously lived only on borrowed phrases, and was nourished only by borrowed thoughts?

33

'Marble Arch,' he said. It was three weeks since he had seen Claire, and he didn't want to think of her. But why, he asked himself, do I persist in searching for that other: that silly nit of a long-haired girl? Why don't I start from another beginning that'll lead to a story without a heroine. Why a girl, when all I know of them is physical? You can't keep on writing about her hair and her legs and all the rest of it, not for more than a chapter anyway.

If not a girl, a boy. No other choice. He'd never liked animals, and couldn't think in abstractions, so it would have to be a boy. He was getting excitedly close to something now, he felt; the relief of discarding the girl and replacing her by a boy was immense. He wasted 9p by getting off before his destination when he saw a large stationer's. The conductress was obviously sorry for him – but only said quietly 'We're not there yet.'

'No, we're not, are we?' he asked, as he got off, 'but we're on our way.'

He waved, but she was pressing the bell, her eyes looking down the bus. He bought a large exercise book, and asked for 250 pages of typing paper, then realised they'd be heavy to lug round the park, and had difficulty in handing the package back and reclaiming his money. Not that she minded, the woman said – it meant nothing to her either way, it was just it kept other customers waiting. As there weren't any other customers, he apologised to them profusely, to a sir, a madam, and a little miss, bending his knees for this one, to look into her little face.

Start with what I know, he said, and mix it with what I wish, and what have we? (a) I know what it's like to be a son. (b) I'd like to have had a father who thought I was brilliant. RIGHT! Go slow, go slow, he mustn't *deserve* it, no

34

that's not the point, the father worships the son and the son accepts it, although everyone else knows he doesn't deserve it. Does the son know too? Obviously the father doesn't . . . does the son know too . . . does the son know . . . that he doesn't deserve . . . ?

He lay on the grass pondering whether the boy knew, and soon he unwrapped the exercise book, and hunted his pockets for a biro. A pencil then . . . any bloody thing that'll write. . . . There had been stacks of biros at that stationer's, he'd even fingered the things – why hadn't he thought . . . He got up off the grass and walked back to Marble Arch, found bewildering difficulty in crossing, and only arrived in something approaching panic on the corner of Great Cumberland Place after ten minutes of dash, retreat, hesitation and sheer inability to move. There was bound to be a stationers here – chemist, hotel, café, Tube station, news-stand, Lyons Corner House . . . he glanced across the road, it looked no more likely there . . . where the hell could he get a pencil – he walked on down Oxford Street past ladies' underwear and ladies' overwear, past shoes, past Marks and Spencers. . . . He was shouting by the time he got to Selfridges. 'A pencil, a pencil, my kingdom for a pencil.' Few people turned to look, though he had raised his voice and his arm theatrically. The West End was used to such outbursts evidently – in North London he would have caused a stir. He spent another five minutes trying to locate a biro in Selfridges, and bought six of them.

'Black,' he said to the girl, 'I'm in mourning.'

'Oh yes,' she said as she bent for a too short paper packet, which she scrumpled round their middles. He put them each in a separate pocket of his jacket, his trousers or his mac, and handed her back the paper.

'You may be needing it,' he said, 'in case you sell a giraffe.'

'A what?' Her face was so naturally blank that it couldn't be said to change to looking more blank; it changed almost imperceptibly to a slight shade more of insolence.

He felt defeated, lonely, shut off from contact with these so many people. But that's what I want, he told himself, I don't want to be part of them, I want to be a loner. And I've got six biros! He set off again for the park, to his surprise picking up the thoughts he wished to think about. Father and son. Over-indulged. Why? Only son? No mother? Best-looking of a brood? Youngest? Talented? No, not really; that was the whole point, the boy mustn't be too gifted, and yet . . . she walked him to school. Had he understood she would leave him – and come back? The concept was difficult. Would the other children be more or less the same? She hadn't spoken her fear to Ed, was he backward . . . in certain things? Would the teachers be all right with him? Should she tell one of them, or would that prejudice them against him? And in fact she might be quite wrong. Some children, many children develop late . . . they say. . . . They soon made it clear he was sub-standard. That is, he could be taught, but he was not quick on understanding, would need a great deal of individual care, et cetera, et cetera. Added to which he was a boorish-looking child, thick-necked, unappealing. But he had moments of tenderness when he would climb on her or Ed's knee, and gently tickle a finger along the contours of their face; and put his kisses on them. That was his own idea, no one had taught him; and at such moments Ed caught his breath with the pain of it. Look at Ed's handsome profile, what strain in my own background has he reverted to . . . he certainly couldn't be treated as . . . sent to a sub-normal school; he has flashes, witty even . . . sometimes makes me laugh.

Now, who the hell would have thought he would think THEM up – who the hell did they think they were anyway, Ed – what an asinine name . . . a five-year-old boy – nothing could be less inviting than a moronic boy – nevertheless, he and his parents had filled his thoughts for the last two hours as he lay on his front, the pad on the grass, the biro alternately in his mouth and on the paper.

He was getting cold; he needed a coffee. Who were they, this Ed and whatsername anyway, what did they want of him, or he of them? And who was she, the one he no longer wanted, the insubstantial vision with the long hair? 'Long hair,' he thought contemptuously. 'What's so special about long hair?'

He crossed to the Edgware Road and to his horror and shame he saw Claire coming towards him. 'I don't want her; she'll get in the way of my thoughts.' He looked nonchalantly across the street, not seeing her, intent on his own life, relaxed, but a small and persistent nob of excitement sat in his diaphragm and with delight and relief he allowed it it's way, and stood to face her as she sauntered towards him. She hadn't seen him. She was swinging her bag which was huge and chocked with the sort of things she thought she couldn't be without: crayons, lavatory paper, old bus and film tickets, a broken mirror, a drawing pad, sticks of charcoal, keys, a railway ticket, postcards of Braques, of Jack Smiths, cotton wool, plasticine, a couple of touch-mice . . . he couldn't remember all the paraphernalia, but he had sat one evening emptying the contents with curiosity, and she had described briefly the necessity for each one in her high tentative voice, and he had dropped them back again.

'Hallo . . .' he said.

They took it for granted that they'd spend the night together, both pretending that the scene at her parents had never taken place, and further that there had not been a parting because of it.

'Got a job?'

'No . . . I've begun the book.'

'Oh, good . . .'

'You?'

She shrugged – 'I want stone, tin, glass, and we're stuck with flat canvas –'

'There's a sculpting class?'

'Next year . . . and with clay. I'm fed up.'

He pinched her thigh. She seemed pleased; it lightened her mood.

Children liked him – he was only a bit backward – when his body grew to match his head he'd be all right. Had they used forceps roughly on bringing him through? She didn't know, had had no other childbirth to compare it with, Ed thought he'd looked a bit odd at the beginning, laughed at it, then he'd got to being soft about him, watching him growing like he was a precious flower. Perhaps they were smothering him too much. He kicked a football all right – bang on – when they went in the park. Got a nice laugh, chuckle – I find myself looking at other people to see if they think we've got an odd one – they never do. And other children like him.

At the school it's doing him good; the teacher said yesterday he's getting on fine – she had been impatient for Ed to come home and be told, and went down the street to meet him, the boy's hand in hers. 'Ed, he's getting on fine the teacher said.' That night they celebrated by going to the local café for ham and chips and tea, all three of them. The next week, or was it the week after, they were in the park and a girl, must have been about eight, threw a ball to him, and Ed and she just sat quiet and watched to see what he would do. He seemed to like her and we all took a cup together across the street, and then, can only have been a matter of weeks later, they asked us over. That started it. They'd got a piano. The girl perched herself on the stool and played a couple of little things, sort of tum-te-tum stuff, and then she sat him on her knee and put his fingers on the notes, and you've never seen such pleasure in a child's face. Well Ed was done for, he'd got to get him a piano no matter what, he knew he said that he had talent, real talent, it only showed a bit at the moment, but even that amount was surprising in a child of five. The Chapmans had been surprised too, got more music in his little finger John Chapman said.

But that just wouldn't do, because he'd have to go on telling the whole story from a woman's, Eva's, point of view if he started like that; and secondly he didn't want to write about the inarticulate. He lived among them for Chrissake; he wanted to *use* words, many words, varying, limpid, evocative words, not over-coined phrases; and Eva and Ed were incapable of anything else. Also, he'd realised, if he wanted the boy to develop the way he'd got in mind, then Ed would have to have money. And Ed was not likely to get any, unless he won the pools which was a more ludicrous supposition for a fictional character even than for anyone else who went in for them. Sorry, Ed and Eva, can't do with you. Unless . . . perhaps Ed could sell insurance?

Yes, but that would take him up and down the country, and he'd got to go to night school and learn all about that music stuff. Maybe this Ed isn't Ed at all but a Jewish type who not only knows about music (his father plays the 'cello and he the violin, and his sister's a pianist) but is rich as well because he's in whatever it is that makes Jews rich. There was a family of Jews in his road, both the father and the son had cars, the mother wore furs . . . father smoked cigars – yah it would be possible, but not if I'm going to write it because I don't know the first thing about them. Why shouldn't Ed and Eva – they were slipping gradually through his fingers – own a grocer's? No – the supermarkets were shutting these people up all over the place – no money in it, at least not down South any more – maybe he should go up North, stay in digs there for a bit, there were wealthy Eds and Evas up there all right – owning shops.

He could take them anywhere; not only place them anywhere (and this was the problem, he hadn't yet decided where to place them either socially or topologically) but he could take them around with him wherever he went . . . or even stay at home with them when he felt like it. The trouble was that nothing he had thought or done since that day in the park had developed them at all. Or altered them; and he wanted to alter them completely but he didn't want to let them in essence go.

What he was certain of and had been since their first appearance was that they were married and had a boy; and he also knew what he and they wanted for that boy. What was holding him back was the business of arranging things for them so that what they wanted would come to pass. Or, looked at the other way, until the father made up his mind how he was going to get enough money to do what he planned to do, Chris couldn't get on with arranging his life for him.

His own life, meanwhile, was slipping to the background of his thoughts, was carrying on its functions without intruding too clearly upon his consciousness. He lived it as a series of cloudy impressions, which no longer jarred on him as something to be borne with set teeth because this was what he was and had; but took its place behind him as a shadow. His father's early morning noises were no more immediate than memories, to be heard or not heard at choice. This was the great solace of the double life – not only could he choose which moments of his characters to think and write about, but he could actually choose which of his own to live, and which to overlay with the thoughts and doings of those others.

And yet the life that occupied his thoughts lacked impetus, was marking time, giving him no pleasure – its compulsion and necessity filling his thoughts with an anxious circular motion, without outlet.

Godlike I can dissolve Ed, create him anew, give him a new name. But with no factual background all that remains is the essence I first suspected of him; his wish, his thought, his ambition, his inner ego, his compulsion to do and be what I had in mind, or what I had in his mind, or what he had in mind for his son, or I had for his son, or I had for him for his son. Eva came white-faced into the room. She'd been to the doctor, only for a check up because Ed had asked her as she seemed so lax lately, so unenergised, so . . . yes . . . uninterested. He had concentrated his love and attention on Tony, talked of him, to him, to the exclusion of her, and in response or revenge she grew less pretty, thin, old-looking; she's probably jealous he told himself, and insisted she had a check up more out of irritation with her inability to bubble, than out of a real consideration for her health. But her face now jolted him out of his easy conviction that whatever she was suffering from was her own fault and 'put on'. Something was evidently and really wrong.

'You'd better talk to him, Ed; he asked if you'd phone.'

'I'll go round and see him. What does he say?' He wanted to say, 'I'm sorry, I know I've been absorbed, but I hadn't really forgotten you, but I haven't the courage to put my arms round you now, because you'll think it's just for comfort; because you're dying . . . Dying!' Was she really dying? 'Oh Christ,' Chris said aloud, 'oh Holy Christ.'

He'd got to save her somehow – couldn't do without her. She was more indispensable to him than she was to Ed, because of . . . no, he didn't want to form into a finished thought yet the part he had in mind for her . . . 'You can't turn down the part now, Eva, old girl,' he said, 'because you're cast, you're an integral part of . . . I *need* you.' He must get Ed and the doctor between them to do something about it. Find a new and miraculous cure for whatever killer disease she was suffering from; or have a second opinion and find the doctor's diagnosis was wrong? Or take her to the sun to recuperate (money again). 'We'll do *something*,' he assured her, 'between us. We all need you. Tony and me especially.' He rubbed his nose up the side of Claire's cheek, then rested it in the warmth of her hair.

'Make me a fetish.'

'A what?' Nevertheless she rummaged for a lump of green stuff and began manipulating. He held out his hand and she gave the whole lump to him, and dipped her arm to the bottom of the bag for some more for herself. He worked the stuff between his fingers, made a ball of it, and dug in his fingernail for eyes, nose, mouth, evoking a possible memory of making a five-year-old's discovery. Why would he get no further with

41

this pliable stuff than this symbolic childish effigy – whereas by juxtaposing thoughts, letters, words, sentences, paragraphs he might be able to reconstitute a man? He gave the head cat's ears, not because he wanted to make a cat but because pulling out those bits was the easiest next thing to do; it was the stuff's own results that reminded him of a cat. He pulled it apart and pressed the stuff into two flat pieces – green coins now; he wrote REX POPULI on them with his nail.

Claire was only practising, finger-limbering, muscle-preparing; this malleable stuff was not her medium, but she would never use it in play as he did, because its purpose for her was a preparation for something else. As Tony won't desecrate his piano with chopsticks . . . or will he? Or would he if Ed weren't listening all the time – or if Ed had ever taught him chopsticks? When Ed went out, which was rare, and left them together with strict instructions to practise hard all the time, she guiltily distracted him, gave him sweets, or played 'touch last' with him; not to disobey Ed, but to counter his driving of the boy; not to mitigate his ambition, but to add the necessary relaxation, and if she were honest to give him a bit of ordinary child's play and see the smile on his face and hear the gurgle of his pleasure. As if she were throwing his medicine down the sink behind the doctor's back, though the medicine would do him good and was not unpleasant to his taste. Most evenings he came back from school, ate his tea and sat for two hours struggling with his notes, patiently re-doing what he was told, repeating a phrase over and over again without seeming to find it either boring or disheartening; blank-faced, his thick unendearing neck turning her heart, his coarse dark hair sprouting rather than growing in odd unmanipulatable directions; behind his ears red where the light spectacle-arms rested. The back view gave no hint ever of the inner child. He was immensely difficult to communicate with; his responses were more like reflexes, lacking core . . . and yet this was what roused her maternal love more than anything.

42

Chris left her watching the child, anxious, fearful, protective –

'Why don't you give it up, and get a job?' he asked Claire.

She didn't answer because she knew he was mimicking others, not asking a question.

Claire demanded very little patience of him – probably instinctively because he possessed hardly any. When Claire disappeared into herself it was to commune with other spirits, not to shut herself away from him into a tight one-self. In fact he realised Claire had it in her to be capable of giving and taking from many people – she would leave him probably as an inessential, whereas he would go on wanting her . . . or would he? 'Don't be honest,' he told himself, 'or you may discover something about yourself you don't want to know.'

Would I murder for money? he wondered. Would I kill Eva to give to Ed? And if she's alive why wouldn't she give it herself? Well, she wouldn't, I know her – or rather I don't, but I know that of her . . . she'll give affection, love, kindness, care, all the help she can, but she won't. . . .

The pianist came brusquely on to the stage, gave a quick bow, sat, and began at once. He played excellently, with a witty vitality; those who were seated were quiet and attentive at once, though about them, and past them, usherettes were still noisily showing latecomers to their seats. Tony was perched forward, hardly on his seat, his mouth open, his whole body tensed. He was wearing huge spectacles, which looked as if they must have been uncomfortable, though he was oblivious of them.

Ed was half-turned towards him, watching the child's reaction, only half concentrating on the music itself, absorbed in the child's absorption. Eva kept her head erect, seemingly listening, but it was obvious that she longed to send swift glances to the child at her side, to know his reaction. She was too well mannered, however, to indulge her wish, and too out of her social element to dare.

43

He was playing the *Apassionata*; Chris's mind mixed and dissolved the material within and without himself, the actuality of the music, phrase by phrase, the rigid attention of the child, the smell of the warm presence of Claire by his side yes I know what all this is leading up to, but it's not valid because . . . and because . . . I know nothing about classical music, and therefore the book will fizzle out after a few pages of notes. This is enough, surely, for despair, but somewhere a nut of hope persists. Why? Was it there in the Festival Hall when we were having coffee, fairly near the beginning, and Claire had said 'But the classic form is dead'? He hadn't caught on at the time, or even really listened, although looking back he remembered a slight passing jolt of surprise. At the time he was more aware of the impression of the memory of her legs, hidden, as he was picturing them, under the table, and the compelling attraction of her sea-green eyes; and his own suffusion of satiated excitement about the music and the performers; his new-found appreciation, the relinquishing of his diaphragm's tightly-drawn knot of disrespectful envy; at the time Claire's remark and her subsequent enlarging on the subject had scarcely intruded on his consciousness, an unnecessary detail of someone else's opinion.

Now, revisualising the scene, the only thing of consequence that was said, thought or felt, was this one vital remark: 'But the classic form is dead.' Or was it 'Classicism is dead' or 'classic music . . .' or . . . no matter; the meaning to him, whatever it had meant to her, was now clear. For him, classicism died the night it was born, fallen in love with and cherished. A one-night love affair. Regretted, remembered, treasured. Dead. His eyes on Claire's fingers (was he talking to her?), he was aware neither of her nor of himself, only that inside him was a ripening, a swelling, without shape or significance but warm with the promise of birth. He need only begin, find a beginning, an opening, and the rest was ready to fall into place, to grow from the first sentence as a living organism grows from a cell. With the imprint of Claire's hands and absorbed head still on his retina, but unable to find its way through the blocked passage to his intelligence he walked out of the house and into the street towards that other life where Ed was working. The room was empty, even spacious; dust sprinkled the floorboards and gathered in dark lumps, drawn together by a common weal perhaps, between the cracks. The skirting was grease on paint on wood, the walls covered with green emulsion. A light bulb, shadeless, hung from the centre of the ceiling, its straggly innards visible. Nothing had been done since they took the place, because, as she agreed, it would take money to make it homely, even habitable. The room adjoining was furnished; cheaply, from what they had each managed to supply when they met. A large bed with a painted headboard; a plywood table with a red cotton sheet on it; a mirror and an ashtray both with the legend British Railway painted round their rims, a thick cord slung across one corner of the room and rawl-plugged (though it was forbidden) into the crumbling plaster, on which were hung a few uninviting male and female clothes . . . but this room was for retiring to, sleeping in, ironing in (there was a plug and an upended iron by it) . . . the other room was for his work. Here he built with anything he could find, it didn't matter what shape, size or colour, the only criterion was that it should not be soft; because when it crashed it must make a distinctive, if not *the* distinctive sound or sequence of sounds that were his life's work. He had had, at the beginning, to be content with the once-only sound, the transient, never-to-be-heard-again noise; but now he had bought a tape-recorder he could keep or erase what he wished, could cut and glue his music – or *Destructo-sculpto* sound as he preferred to call it – to produce one sound immediately after another, or gauge exactly how long each silence should be, instead of, as in the old days, having to depend on how quickly he could build again to destroy.

He seldom kept any of the paraphernalia for more than half a dozen buildings, except a bicycle bell without a top, and a handleless green-and-rust dustpan. The rest of the things sometimes after being used only once, he threw into the communal dustbin outside the multi-inhabited house.

The first revelation of sound had come to Ed at eight years old during the war, when he had heard, actually heard with his whole musical being, the orchestration of what was going on around him, the drone of the planes a sustained note of terrifying background. He waited for, and at last heard, the deafening crash of the solo instrument, the falling falling terminal bomb. The pause was held, and then came not the wailing of the wind instruments, but the tiny mew of a day-old child. Eddie had stayed awake, breathless, for the hours of silence which followed, hugging the symphony to him for fear of forgetting it; and as early as he dared, perhaps three hours later when a finger of light had seeped through the corner of the blackout, he could wait no longer, but got out of bed and re-orchestrated the whole thing. He held the drone, like a bee-buzz on his lips, renewing his breath as surreptitiously as he could to give the impression of that long-drawn-out note from the full but distant orchestra. Then, at the climactic moment he had compulsively seized the chair, the only possible instrument in the room, and hurled it against the mirror which splintered with a wonderful unlooked-for sound to the wooden floor. He held his breath for delight and wonder, and for the exact space of the musical silence he wanted, and then, crumbling to the floorboards, he let out the tiny, slender, palely-dying mew.

'Frightening your mother like that.'

'Waking us up – God knows, we've had little enough sleep.'

'Isn't the raids bad enough, but you have to go and make them frightening noises too?'

'Thought the roof was coming in.'

'What'll the neighbours say?'

'Naughty boy.'

'Get back to bed.'

'Give us a bit of peace.'

No one had ears to hear. 'Making them frightening noises.' No one wanted to re-create sound, or assemble it without re-assemblage, for its own sake and immediacy.

'Naughty boy.'

So he kept his hearing to himself, delighting in it, hugging it to him surreptitiously, ashamedly, because it was a secret naughtiness; an evil compulsion.

He was never considered musical at school; at home he was never considered.

Radio music bored him, the unstimulating background wail and repeat of daily grind there to dim and dull the pain of being alive in this deathly war; grown-ups, his mother particularly, indulged in it endlessly; it was impossible for him to tell her how its deadliness pained him. His ears couldn't ignore it as hers could. This was what pleased her about it, though he noticed that she noticed the emptiness of its absence. When he could stand it no longer he would amble as if unconsciously, acting it out for her sake, to twist and turn the knobs at the side.

He found excruciating delight in the atmospheric shrieks the knobs unveiled between stations.

'Put that thing on or off.'

'Stop fiddling about.'

He desisted, and put his head out of the window – traffic; rumble, punctuated by shrieks, blasts and that blessed speed-noise, which took the place of speed itself, of the new Lambrettas. He would own one one day, its throb was one of the highest musical excitements to him. His own child, re-sembling him physically and therefore he hoped aurally, would be encouraged, even beaten if need be, into hearing, re-hearsing, creating, re-creating, the sound of sound. Or so he had thought, those twenty odd years ago.

And yet when the child was born, and later proved back-ward, he gave up this idea and concentrated on forging his own sound, leaving Eva to cope with this creature who had let down his dreams. Now and then he would use the childish noises, off-stage as it were, half-heard, irrelevant; strangely he never thought of the child's very inarticulateness as of value. Not, that is, until the boy was about five.

'Come on in here.'

'Oh, Ed, he's just getting off to sleep.'

'Tony! Come on in here. Do as I tell you.'

'And it's cold, Ed, I've only just got him comfortably warm.'

'Look, I haven't worked for days, and now I've found some-thing. Make him come in.'

'No, Ed. . . .'

That he had started work again did touch her. It was the mainspring of his life. She hesitated now; torn between the need to help him and the need to let Tony sleep and be warm. 'Oh . . . Ed. . . .' She stood irresolute in the doorway between the room where they lived and slept and the work-room; the struggle even. 'You get him, I haven't the heart,' she finally said, and irritated by her non-co-operation, and by her sup-port, love and bourgeois devotion of feeding, caressing, warm-ing and appeasing, he pushed past her, and pulling back the covering, grabbed his upper arm, transferring her refusal to the boy's, angry with him for her denial, sure now that it was Tony who had said no.

He did indeed say no now, loud and long in a deep grown-up drill-hall rasp, as he was dragged from thumb-sucking death-like lovely unconsciousness into 'there', his vest not long enough to cover his genitals, nor the flaking white skin of his thighs, to stand at the ready by the conglomerate mass of 'things' his father had built, and wait for the hand-signal which meant 'now' when he Tony must push over the this and the that, giving it another shove if it didn't all fall. Three

48

times he closed his eyes and hung his head in a stupid imita-
tion of standing sleep, unable to see the raised hand lowered;
three times Ed whispered 'This time, this time, now, now' in
growing but contained excitement as the moment of destruction neared; three times Ed switched the tape-recorder on
and angrily off again as no sound of movement came. The
fourth time, in despair as the cold held his body in iron
rigidity, with a wounded-to-death animal cry, Tony pushed
and pushed, and howling with rage and the loss of the battle
as well as the loss of sleep, ran past his mother to find the now-
cold bed and the callus on his thumb.

Eva undressed and got into bed herself, without comment-
ing on the performance, or looking into the work-room. Her
underlying motive was to get him to sleep now with the
warmth of her body; not in defiance of Ed but with the sickening knowledge that the position her nature had compelled her
to take had made both her husband and her child losers. She
had neither saved Tony from the cold, not offered Ed her sup-
port, and in acting as she had she had temporarily lost the love
and trust of both. As she would always do. She knew that she
took sides; in the plural, now one, now the other, now both
together, and wherever her weight went each of them would
always believe that she took the other side, and left *them*
alone, cold and despairing. To Tony both parents had connived to make him miserable. She had stood by watching him
being dragged from bed; had closed the door on him and not
watched his misery, and allowed him without a word of con-
solation to return ice to ice. He refused to forgive her until the
warmth of her arms and belly enveloped him in drowsiness,
and he accepted the warm lips on the back of his ear. To Ed,
alone now that the sound had happened and like an orgasm
was released from him, leaving no further desire until the next
creative compulsion should seize him, she had unashamedly
and strongly sided against him, and he felt himself unfairly
isolated from her approbation. 'She makes a pretence of

understanding – but her whole nature is closed, tight, unap-prehending. I must make my way alone. The moron and she against me.' He too eventually got into bed, muscles tensed to hold himself away from her body.

She turned to him; 'Pretending because the boy is now asleep and she has no need to appease him further. So now she turns her attention to me, but no thank you, I'm not such easy prey.' Nevertheless after an hour his compassion for her won, and he forgave her, intertwining his cold legs and thighs with her warm ones.

At the thought of warm thighs Chris looked up. Claire was in bed, sleeping on her back, tousled, childish-looking. His own legs, cold as Ed's, felt weak, longed for her. He looked at the clock. Twenty past three . . . no wonder he felt cold . . .

Sunday they lay in bed late. The boy made noises, hummed a low zoo-oom sound; his fingers crossing and recrossing the air. He was sitting up cross-legged in his vest, not noticing the cold, now that Ed wished he'd lie down and shut up. Per-verse little moron. Can't really use the word 'little' – a com-passionate word . . . the word he needed was squat, but for some reason the language didn't lend itself to 'perverse squat moron' . . . it needed the double syllable of 'little'. She'd get up of course in a minute in case the squat moron was hungry. Would she have been less or more attentive if he'd been attractive, normal . . . would I? Yes, I would, I'd have taken him for walks, talked to him, taught him . . . made him listen to the sound. Of sound. The deep need for a son, he realised now, had been the mainstay of his childhood, 'When I have a son, I won't treat him like this,' had suffused his mind and body. His prayer (if prayer means a wish that is more important than the sort of thing one would wish if one chose the right piece of chicken bone), prayer? No, that wasn't the word, 'longing' was nearer . . . his hoping for a son had been granted – but like the story of the Monkey's Paw it had turned out to be a macabre joke. How could he treat this child as he wished he'd been treated by *his* parents. It was insensitive. He couldn't approach it. A son as he had dreamed him would have shared in his longing, would have destroyed with him, would be part of here and now; not a freakish backward-looking numbskull. He put from him the thought that they might have another. No thank you. One mistake was enough. It tied you for life. It altered your relationship with your wife. It made you suspect that they suspected *you* of faulty genes. For months Ed had believed that his own physical disability, the limp, resulting from the night when he had been buried under all that debris (his parents had been out at the time: 'Naughty boy, I *told* you to go to the shelter'), had been transferred to his offspring. But instead of voicing his guilt and misery to Eva he had searched through medical books in the library, and eventually proved to his own satisfaction that a future generation is not at all affected by the acquired physical disabilities of its parents. An accident did not alter the genes, the genes were what transmitted themselves. He was satisfied, but he was not relieved. He still felt the guilt to be his, and for this reason was irrationally inclined to blame Eva.

'Squat moron,' he said aloud in his disappointment. 'Oh Ed . . . don't.' She was always shocked when he spoke the obvious aloud. 'You're dishonest,' he told her, 'with yourself.' But she no longer got hurt as she had done when he first voiced the misery. She spoke now out of bourgeois shock, that one 'doesn't say such things,' that one doesn't face them. 'Oh Ed . . . don't' had become almost mechanical, as if her only necessity now was to tell him he was wrong. And yet, he knew she was still necessary to him, and beautiful, beautiful. How could that plump young body have produced *that*: and why did those exquisitely rounded feminine arms cuddle *that* with such warmth and delight? And how could those deep green eyes retain, as they did, the laughter that had first astounded him, and then become his anchor? He could make her cry – often did . . . but she knew that what he really wanted was the answering laughter at life and its miseries. He humped over and lay on her, gazing into the greenness, pressing his leaness on her rounded warmth. She pursed her mouth: 'Oh ... Ed.'

The boy continued his 'zoom-zoom' cross-legged on the bed – his parents' rhythmical humping made no intrusion on his concentration on the repetition of an arm-movement accompanied by a drawn-out sound.

They stayed in bed till midday, then she fried some sausages, which they ate hot and grease-dripping, between slices of white bread. She put new trousers on the boy – long ones, in grey and yellow check; autumn had come and she'd got them cheap. They wandered out, crossed Shepherd's Bush by the track, to buy a newspaper on the other side of the Green. It was early enough to find two places on a bench. She had bought chewing-gum. They chewed and read together, *The News of the World*, she looking over his arm as he held it spread. Now and then small gusts of wind pushed or crumpled the page, wilfully undetermined as to which way to blow. The boy strode her outstretched thigh, chewing contentedly. He had on his old knitted wool cap that kept his ears warm. After a bit he stood up, obviously intent, his back held in interest; she followed his gaze – to a ball, and a girl with greasy fair hair, about eight years old; behind the girl she thought she recognised ... yes it was. ...

'Ed, on that bench there.'

'What?' He read slower than she did, was not yet ready to turn to page nine. She was interrupting a juicy bit.

'That's my boss. Chapman.'

'So?'

'Don't you want to see what he looks like?'

'Later. Shut up a bit can't you?'

The little girl turned round, and seeing Tony's absorbed face held out the ball to him at once.

'Put your hands up!' she called in a high strident voice;

and gently aimed to get the ball near him. He didn't put up his hands, he had never played with a ball, but he scrambled after it with more speed and resolution than he had as yet shown, and retrieved it from under the bench. He went shyly towards her offering it.

'Throw it!' she shrieked.

He stood and let it fall for her to come and take.

'*That's* it,' she said encouraging him. She ran for it, picked it up, showing him how to place his hands together, took some paces back, and aimed again. The boy was laughing, the noises he made when tickled.

'It's Chapman, Ed. The girl's his. The one talking to Tony.'

'Well, what do you want to do about it?'

'Yes it is him. That's his mother with him. That's her hat.'

'Well, give them a nod if you want to.' He bent back the paper with difficulty, tried turning to page nine, the wind was blowing in the wrong direction to achieve it. He stood up, turned to face the wind, and felt he'd cheated it when in this position he found that the paper folded easily.

Tony was right by the Chapmans now, and the girl was aiming the ball between his legs.

'Come and meet them. We'll have to.'

He followed her slowly, towards the bench.

The woman called, 'Look who's here, then . . . from the shop.'

'Bit cold,' said Chapman. 'Care for a cuppa?'

'I'm starved,' said his mother. 'Let's go and warm up, yes?'

'Can he come?' the girl asked.

'Of course he's coming, Bridget.'

Perhaps no one had noticed. If only he behaved himself, didn't wet his pants. She should ask them back really, but she wouldn't dare. What would they make of the work-room, and Ed's stuff, and she hadn't made the bed either in the other room, and the frying-pan and lard et cetera was still all over the place.

53

In spite of the cold day they ambled because Chapman's mother walked more sideways than forwards, so that progress along the pavement was slow.

'That's it.' Chapman pointed his thumb at a darkened shop window, he put his key, however, not into the shop door, but a narrow entrance at its side. The door opened on to a steep flight of steps.

'Come on up.'

'Oh, can't we play in the shop!'

'I'm not lighting up, not on a Sunday.'

'We don't neeed light.'

'Don't knock anything over, Bridget!'

'No . . . I know where everything is. I want to show him the rocking-horse and the great bear.'

Chapman was a soft-eyed man in his early fifties; pale-skinned, perhaps from illness, or perhaps spending time among old things had desiccated him.

His wife had left him when the child was eighteen months old, gone off with a black. Not primarily for love, but because intellectually she couldn't stand Chapman's aversion, which was not masked. She did it to 'show him' and to show 'them' and now he supposed she had dark babies and felt intellectually the better for it. All this Eva had heard from him in fragments over the months, standing in the shop; she hadn't talked of him to Ed because she knew it wouldn't interest him. This 'antique' shop had very little that was before 1900, but a lot of accumulated junk since that date. The place was full of enjoyable, useless things, the less useful the more Chapman liked them.

Over the shop front was written in thick once-gold characters on municipal green E. & R. PENGE *Antique Dealers.* Chapman, when he had bought the shop, had simply left the lettering there as he might have done had it been the name of a house on a garden gate. He was L. Chapman, E. & R. Penge, 121 Cambridge Road, Chiswick, W.4.

Inside, the shop was a narow deep affair with largish recesses on either side, and contained things both hideous and lovely, huge and tiny, worthless and valuable, comparable to the many other junk-shops to be found in and around the centre of London. Most of the once valuable things were now either broken, cracked, or had parts missing; these mishaps having turned them in a second from antiques into junk.

In one of the recesses was an earless rocking-horse, mounted, not on rockers but on a black iron stand fixed to its belly; strained in that galloping position necessary to all one-time merry-go-round horses. He still rocked, but with an erotic up-and-down movement, unlike the back-and-forth rock of a household toy.

It was here that Bridget had brought Tony, and had with difficulty heaved him on to the beloved beast.

'Lovely,' Tony said. It was the first time he had uttered the word, and the fact that he was communicating at all would have both amazed and shocked his parents.

'Lovely,' responded Bridget, who understood him easily, having only three years earlier quitted being five years old.

'Love-lee,' said Tony.

'Lovy – lovy – lee,' she responded, one hand reaching to his knee the other stretched to hold him by the elastic waist on the back of his trousers.

'Lee love.'

'Lee – lee – lee – lee.'

The possibilities of the distortion of the word were never-ending, for the delightful reason that one could repeat any one of them, there was no need to search for a new combination of letters. Also there were (it was Tony who discovered them) a hundred possibilities of calling the word in different keys, or different tones of voice. From ecstatic to mock horror, to the toppest screech they could manage to the lowest depths their vocal chords could touch. The game might have gone on till Ed or Eva interrupted with a come-along we're going home,

had not Bridget, inspired, gone to the broken legged piano
and sung 'Love – lee' 'Lover – lover – lover' whilst hitting
the highest and lowest notes the old instrument was capable
of. Tony held his body rigid on the horse, caught his breath
and held that too, then fearlessly, scrambled off the horse and
ran to her. She hit a few notes to show him. Then she played
her 'piece', 'Gliding down the river', then she showed him
chopsticks; then she moved over and let him stand in front of
it. He pounded. Both hands open, palms down, fingers wide.
He banged. The thing responded. A girl and a piano had responded to him in one day, opening whatever gates had
hitherto been closed and locked inside him. He shouted,
he banged, now and then he tickled one note by itself, then
two, then two in each hand. It responded each time, magically,
differently. It was while he was in the midst of this bang-
shout-tickle ecstasy, that the inevitable words came: come-
on-we're-going-home. Neither of the children paid any
attention. Bridget replayed her 'Gliding down the river'
while he continued to experiment.

'Very good, boy,' called Ed. He advanced slowly and
leaned on the piano facing him, watching the effect on the boy
of the magic of making his own sound. The results were not
looked for, any more than Ed's own; he too simply did something, and the result came of itself, inevitably, connived by
him, but without his plan or foreknowledge. The whole of Ed's
mind and body concentrated into one swelling of what this
pleasure in the son might mean to the father. It impinged on
his creative consciousness that a piano was not, as he had supposed, an outdated sentimental harmony-recording piece of
antiquity, but a possible vital part of Destructo-music. The
orgasmic completion of his life, he felt, might even be the
destruction of this particular piece of material. He wetted his
lips with the pleasure of the anticipation, the straining and
pulling out of the guts, the hammering out of the keys, the
splintering of the wood. He imagined it many different ways;

but its actual moment he would defer, in case and because after such a high moment of his art he might never reach or even wish to reach such creative competition again.

'I haven't been wasting my time!' he said to himself, unaware until this moment that he had thought that he had.

'Come along, Tony love,' said Eva, as if the heavens had not moved; indeed as if nothing at all of import had happened. She was still living in the past, that past of five minutes ago when between their love-hate relationship there loomed this child that she must protect and he must bully. He was not going to let her stand in the way; she would have to live life as *he* willed it now, and as Tony would will it. He wouldn't explain anything to her. Indeed, what was there to explain that could be shaped into an explanation? All it meant was that he would make sure every minute of his life from now on that Tony's life was shaped to Tony's ends. The ends were as yet in a vague and huge mist in Ed's mind, but in the mist there lurked the eternal dream.

'Wasn't he extraordinary?' she said, when they got home.

He didn't want to share his own awareness of Tony's potential.

'How do you mean?' he said.

'Well, with the girl . . . behaving like that . . . everything . . . just . . . ordinary.'

He said: 'He's always been all right but you've never allowed him to be. Always doing everything for him – you've never given him a chance.'

'Oh . . . Ed.' Did he really believe she had stood in the way of his progress? And as if to confirm it, she remembered in the school cloakroom when she was bending to tie up his shoelace, the girl who looked after them when they weren't in class had said: 'You spoil him.'

Eva's first reaction had been the wish to slap her face. But now she confronted herself with its possible truth, in the light of Ed's accusation. But I know they're both wrong. Unless I say 'Do you want the cloakroom?' he'll hold it in till he wets himself even though I've *told* him. I've explained again and again. I've even threatened. And I've offered rewards, sweets, if he'll tell me in time. But he won't or can't. So what am I to do except spoil him by reminding him everyday? I've tried; Ed's tried, he *must* remember saying 'Put your vest on' and what happens? He stands and gets cold, and if he's shouted at he cries. Same thing. Every time. So isn't loving him and caring for him right, even under the name of spoiling? The mistress says he's not sub: 'Just lazy, not very bright, but they wouldn't accept him in an E.S.N. school. He's not under average enough, and this sort of child can develop. It often comes from difficulties at home.' That was the other accusation, that she and Ed together were somehow in their behaviour responsible for his backwardness. But what had they done? And would he have *looked* so backward at six months old with that huge head and the hair that wouldn't grow, but sprouted in tufts, if he'd been o.k. in himself, and just distorted by them? Ed was hard with him, yes, and she was soft, but that was the usual way with parents who brought up perfectly normal children. It seemed that whatever natural re-action she had was suspect. And not only to that young schoolteacher, but to Ed too. If she tried to protect him, she left him wide open to Ed's anger; if she tried to remain neutral and leave their relationship to themselves their dislike of each other fermented. And yet she recognised her inter-ference as spiritual clumsiness; and had deduced that this thickness in her nature had transmitted itself to her son's body. She didn't admit this aloud to Ed, but she sensed that he knew, and blamed her. Ed on the contrary had never had any such thought. His sole concern was that she be free of the imposition and weight of the child, who was ageing her, and destroying the beauty that was his touchstone; the still centre from which all the panic and horror and disgust and thrill and vitality and sense of destruction could emanate. Without her as a centre and proof of continuity and permanence how could he create chaos and dissolution? If there were no Evas, the ugliness of life itself would be self-evident, would not need his art to proclaim it. While she existed, he must disturb, destroy.

The boy was tired from a bodily sense of having been alive, awake, and he slept deeply and totally from the moment she lay him in bed. She went to the work-room, she needed to talk about him, to delight in him with Ed, and of course, guiltily, she needed to make sure that Ed did not disturb that necessary and blissful depth of sleep. She was conscious of cheating as she began . . . 'Wasn't it a surprise?' 'Aren't you pleased . . . ?' 'Isn't it good?' She didn't choose a sentence, said all three and more without conveying any more than one would have done. He suspected her; but in any case his desire to build and destroy had been roused earlier. He left her standing in his work-room and went through to the bedroom, closing the door on her behind him.

'Tony,' he said gently, almost beseechingly. 'Tony.' The back of the head only was visible. He went over to the bed, sat on it by him, and rhythmically shook him. No reply, the movement being a rocking, deepened and pleasured the boy's sleep. Ed didn't want to shout, to let her know what he was doing. There was no water in here to sprinkle over the boy, the washbasin was in the work-room, invaluably there, since the noise of running water could continue to sluice or drip at the end of each destructive exercise, leaving an impression of eternal gush or of a pointless, piddling forever. He remembered a trick from his childhood, when his mother used to wake him. She would pass her fingers over his forehead in a seeming caress, which had the power to waken not only his slumbering consciousness, but the depths of his most terrified soul. What hideous and unspeakable memories were aroused with those horrors . . . but the touch had done the trick. If he used it now on Tony, it had the advantage of seeming-kindness, even to himself – how could he be expected to remember its awful result? And also it would not alert Eva in the next room, holding her breath no doubt, in wait for the dreaded shriek.

Tony opened his eyes at the touch and revealed in their depths, and behind the structure of his whole face, such a horror as only madmen could keep in their subconscious. Ed was reminded painfully of his own tortured wakings, but attempted to stifle the cries that would inevitably come when the being realised that he was awake, and only dimly apprehended what terrors he had left behind.

'Would you like me to buy you a piano?' he whispered. But the boy could only live on one track at a time, had not the agility to replace agony with pleasure, at a sentence. He prepared his face and lungs for a bawl. Ed put the pillow sharply across him, held ready for this emergency, and lying down with him, the pillow covering both their heads, he whispered, stroking the boy's arm, shoulder, thigh, 'A piano for Tony. Like the little girl played. Tony can have that piano. Dada will buy Tony the little girl's piano.' But Tony didn't wish to remember his joy now; that belonged to another time. Now all he wanted was to be left alone, to find again the unconsciousness of sleep, to be left alone . . . alone. Ed got up off the bed and gently covered him. All his desires were likely to bear fruit. They would work together from now on. Tremendous rushes of future sound diffused him. He couldn't remember ever having been so happy, so near his heart's desire, so near creation. But so secure was this desire now that it could wait. He needn't after all wake him tonight. There would be a lifetime of work, not just one rush of uninhibited destruction. He could make love to Eva, go to work, walk along the streets, without fear and misery now, because the kingdom of heaven was at hand within him, in a glorious religious knowledge of the power of destruction.

He looked dispassionately at the now sleeping boy, then opened the door quietly. Eva was caught in a moment of aloneness that had not thought to be surprised into being looked at. How much older and less secure her lone self was than the one that walked with others . . . he was as surprised as the one he had surprised. She adjusted her expression to one of relief, and tenderness.

'O.k.?' she said. He put his arms round her and kissed her warmly, strongly, with the love that she had not felt in him since she had presented him with the monstrous offspring.

She dropped him at the school too early on the Monday, to get to work before Chapman left. But he'd gone already on his usual two-day tour and wouldn't be back till Wednesday morning. The piano wasn't priced, probably wasn't even for sale, was kept there for Bridget perhaps. Nor come to think of it was the rocking-horse marked, not that she wanted to buy him *that*. Ed would simply have him falling off it and with it until both were broken.

She let herself into the side door as usual, prepared to unlock the shop door and its gates from the inside. There was a note this morning. Not unusual. 'Mother staying upstairs, can you do midday shopping? Cut-loaf. Bag of chips. Six eggs. Thank you. C. Chapman.'

They paid her for keeping the objects dusted, polishing the silver and brass ones, and keeping shop. More often than not she did the shopping for him in her lunch hour. She didn't mind. It was convenient work, near the school, Chapman fitted in with her hours, and anyway she liked junk, it was appealing. Upstairs too was full of useless and ugly bric-à-brac, lovely to Eva's eyes, who would have adorned her bedroom with anything she could find had Ed allowed her to.

Before unlocking the shop she went upstairs and opened the flat door with the spare key, knocking as she did so, which was her custom.

'Mrs Chapman?'

'In here.'

'Anything else you want?'

Mrs Chapman was in bed propped on a bolster, blind-looking without her glasses which had protected the dark brown sludgy eyes for so many years. She sucked saliva into her teeth in irritation – 'Didn't he leave you the note then?'

'Oh yes, I just wondered . . . oh, and someone was enquiring yesterday whether . . .'

'Yesterday? Sunday?'

'No, it must have been Friday then . . . whether the piano isn't for sale, I mean how much the piano is.' Why on earth was she telling a lie instead of straightforwardly stating that Ed wanted to buy the piano? Was it that she feared Mrs Chapman's unprotected eyes? Or was she ashamed in some way that Ed wanted the piano, and was unnecessarily protecting him? Or was it that she thought the piano wouldn't be for sale for her, because she was not a customer, but only someone who worked for them? More likely it was the fear that their attitude towards their child's banging yesterday might be laughed at. A monkey could hit a piano as well as Tony had, it was not likely that the Chapmans would understand why this ability had meant so much to Ed.

'It's not got the price on it?'

'No.'

'Then it's not for sale.'

'But if it was offered for?'

'Maybe, it would depend how much was offered, don't forget the eggs will you, we're out of them.'

Now should I say the customer has offered seven pounds for it and see what happens? she wondered as she went down to the shop. Or should I wait a bit and say the customer hasn't come back, but I myself would offer seven quid for it, and see the reaction? I'll have to wait till Chapman's back, can't get any further with her. Ed'll be livid with me, when he wants something he wants it now. Well he can't have it and that's that. What about other pianos? There're lots of junk shops only a bus-ride away. . . .

She went downstairs, took off the bric-à-brac from the lid of the piano and the silk tasselled shawl and opened the piano lid. One coil of wire lay limply among the stretched ones, a corpse among the living, and only a few of the hammers had felt on them. She touched the keyboard quietly, 'She'll think I'm dusting it' . . . and, leaning over, watched the reaction of the hammers. Some notes played not at all, and had no effect inside. Some belonged to their inner workings. She hastily closed it all, put back the silk mantle, the candlesticks, the china toad, the leather blotter and the rest of the things.

No one came in before lunch, though a couple, and later on an old man, picked up some of the prints she'd arranged outside on the two oak chairs.

At lunch she had a cheeseburger and coffee sitting up at the bar of the café next door to where Ed worked. She wouldn't have dreamed of lunching where he served – it would have seemed to them both shameful and somehow dishonest. Nor did she ever glance through the window to see him there in his white coat. She bought an *Evening Standard*. There were two advertisements for pianos in the 'for sale' column. One was for £45 'in excellent condition' and the other '£70 or nearest'. Of course they couldn't afford them. She wondered what price Ed would go up to. Seeing he'd set his heart on one, where his work was concerned he was ruthless. She recognised his sound-making as his work, and his job as a waiter in a café as only a necessary way of staying alive until his work itself should be recognised and in some way paid for. She had day-dreams of recording companies offering him large contracts, of she herself standing outside the B.B.C. waiting for him to come out after rehearsal. To him his work was above his well-being. She had never made the mistake of disturbing him in his work to offer him food. Well, she'd have to tell him tonight of her failure to get a price for the piano in the shop until

Wednesday; and show him that she'd even been serious about it and bought a *Standard*.

She felt that pain again – now what had she eaten last night. Or at lunch. The cheeseburger of course, they always said cheese gave you indigestion.

Ed had always set himself a two-hour working morning, from eight-thirty when the other two left for school and shop, till it was time to go to the café and set out the tables for lunch. He began by cutting and rearranging yesterday's tape; spent a short while out of doors prowling among local dustbins for possible new material; came home to listen, once only, to the tape, and began . . . but only began . . . building a new edifice. He had a three-hour break in the afternoon but it was disrupted by the boy being brought home from school and given tea, and by Eva doing her desultory housework. After tea was the most difficult time to get either Tony to work with him, or her to co-operate, so he had no alternative but to wake the boy when he came in from the café around eleven at night.

He would limp springily back home along the pavement and across Shepherd's Bush, his mac unbuttoned, the mike held before him like an offered flower catching the traffic of night, carrying with him a bodily desire akin to a sexual imperative, excitedly saving and savouring it until he could get home, rearrange the construction of the morning, face Eva's remonstrances, wake the boy, and finally, through torment and frustration, achieve (as he always did with enough persistence and ruthlessness) the orgasmic sound of the conglomerate descent.

What he was planning now, however, was a longer-term project, during which his desires must be mingled with an excruciating patience, worth while he knew, because he already felt inside his diaphragm the possibility of outcomes more rich and daring than anything he had been able to create before; partly, he admitted, because of his lack of inspiration, partly, he suspected, because until now his talent had not matured.

His job at the café was not wasted time. He had never al-

64

lowed it to become a job for its own sake or for the sake of money. He had always with him the recorder and tape which he expunged with each new sound each new day keeping only the heightened moments which seemed to him to have absolute merit. Plates, cups, spoons, voices, trays performed for him, as did the traffic and the days' extraneous sounds, as did his own footsteps.

In the café the mike hung inside his waiter's light-weight white coat, its wire passing up the sleeve and down inside his jacket to the pocket where the recording machine and the tapes nestled. His boss had never referred to it. In fact, he thought it was either a deaf aid or possibly some form of help for the crippled walk. Having switched back and played over a day's recording, Ed preferred to expunge it by overlaying it with the next day's. What was past was dead. There was little point in bringing it forward into the present except for those odd moments which had the power to rekindle their own life by mixing unexpectedly with something from their future, or with some Ed-created moment poised and waiting for them. Balance was the great thing. Or rather Imbalance. The Imbalance of the properties of chosen sounds, themselves haphazard and of no one's conscious choice held a great appeal for him, if they held within them the destructive element. Sometimes, very rarely, incongruous destruction-sounds registered themselves without his aid; the most humorous being a roar of tumbling sand from a building site, a shrieking unoiled brake of a lorry and, as accompaniment in sweet stupidity, the distant sound of a church bell. This recording had been all the more fascinating to him, because he had at the same time caught one of his own un-prearranged reactions, a giggle-snort of satisfaction, made, though he wasn't aware of doing it, down his nose.

This Monday he hurried his free lunch at the café, the leftovers of stew, a good helping of potatoes and a large cup of coffee, and went home eagerly to await Eva's news of the price of the piano. Apart from the few pounds he had spent

65

over a couple of years ago on the cassette, and two tapes, he had had no outlay on his musical work. He had a post office savings account of, he supposed, over £1000 but he would have to augment this into being an adequate supply for Tony's predictable future, not spend it now.

He got home well before Eva and the boy, but didn't feel like work. His impatience took him down to the pavement and back three or four times to see if they were coming.

'You're early,' she said. 'Did you put the kettle on?'

'Well, how much is it then?'

'It's not priced.'

'Didn't you *ask*?'

'It's Monday.'

'So?'

'He doesn't get back till Wednesday morning. I bought a *Standard*, but they're too much.'

Later she said: 'If he asks, what price shall I say . . . ?'

'You don't have to say it's for us.'

'No, I won't; I know. I can say someone has asked.'

He didn't reply so she said again: 'How much shall I say they've said?'

'Seven quid. Suggest seven quid.'

'All right then . . .'

He switched on and listened . . . crockery . . . voices . . .

'I'll wipe it all,' he said, 'there's nothing worth saving.'

'Couldn't you keep *something*?' Not that she really minded, she simply wanted to show him that she valued what he'd already done.

'You haven't got the point *yet* have you,' he said.

'I only thought. . . .'

'The whole *point* of my sound is that it's not non-enduring. It exists once. Like you. Like him. Like me. ONCE. How can you interpret a non-enduring universe by enduring, or recorded, sound?' He waited. She had her head down, silent, over her plate, then he said, 'H'm?' twice.

66

'We're not unenduring,' she ventured very quietly. She was shy, he'd never discussed such things before.

'Who're not? What is not?'

'Us. You. Me.'

'Are you eternal then?'

'No, of course, not. But I last for a bit. A bit of time. Some years in fact.'

'You won't. Nothing will. The earth won't. . . .'

'Well, for a bit . . .' she said, quite out of her depth.

'Well, my sound lasts for a bit doesn't it? Until I've heard it or at any rate until it has proclaimed itself – I let it come to birth don't I? In the future I may not even do that.'

'But you said there isn't a future.'

'I'm talking relatively. I should have said from now on.'

'Then why do you want a piano?'

'All right then, we won't have the bloody piano.'

They were on firm well-known ground now. She would want the piano for Tony's sake, and he would withhold it. Not from the boy; from himself. Because no one understood.

'I didn't say I didn't want the piano.'

'It's all right. I don't mind. I certainly am not going to buy one now.'

'But I'd like one, Ed.'

'I've told you the subject is closed.'

She started to cry: 'Why can't we have one?'

'Whatever I suggest is wrong,' he muttered, 'whatever I want you don't think is right. All right, you win.'

She went into the bedroom to get over the frustration she felt, and to stop him seeing the tears.

'Come on, let's build together,' he said to the boy, quietly, in control. 'Come and help.'

He placed the boy's hands on the table, and standing behind him, his hands on the child's, his legs striding outside the boy's legs, he shoved both table and boy before him, to the corner of the room.

'No, no, put the mug back. Good boy. We'll need that. Now, what shall we put next?' The boy was responding beautifully – without fear and with more purpose than he'd shown before. They built up the things from the room gradually, not all of them, but most; at the top was lain flat the bicycle wheel. The boy could not reach up to the top now. but he half-wheeled, half-tumbled it for Ed to place. 'All very well,' thought Ed, 'but before I switch on I'm going to want a bit of raucous rebellion, otherwise there's no point.' The Universe must not crumble without human protest, it was the protest that mattered, the cry, the rage against the finale, the never-to-be-repeated experiment. As a prelude he made great show of placing the mug high.

'No, no, no,' said Tony, but it was not in panic, simply a negative, a difference of opinion about using or not a mug.

'Right then, it's yourself.' He heaved the boy to the top of the pile, only six foot up or so, but death's height to Tony who started at once his panicked remonstrances. Ed switched on. If he missed the beginning the build-up was never so exciting, so complete, and if she should come in now it would add to the effect, as she knew, which was always a source of indecision to her. Should she protest and therefore give him the effect he wanted and in consequence make certain that he would use Tony and her protest again? Or not protest and spoil (though only very slightly) his total effect, and at the same time leave her boy to suffer alone? She came. He got the click of the door, the moan of fear as Tony half-fell with the edifice into her arms, her voice saying stupidly 'It's all right, darling,' when it quite patently was not; and this time even the tack, tack, of dripping water from the sink, as she faced him wordlessly, and he concentrated with his ears, his finger ready to switch off.

What he had not yet resolved, but which was always in his thoughts, was a technique whereby the 'once only' phenomenon should be really and truly once only. As it was now, the taping of destruction was the once and the replaying of many

68

destructions together was a repeat. There was also the difficulty of editing so that at no moment would the edifice sound as if it had been re-erected. This contradiction must be wiped out altogether, so that each destruction became one, and together, one total, because destruction followed by re-construction was against all that he wanted to express.

'I could look in other shops tomorrow,' she said, in a low conciliatory tone, whilst her hands comforted the child. He recognised speech as the second-best of her offerings; the physical ones nearly always put the child first. He was conscious of being fobbed off with pretended concern.

'Or *you* could. Why not try the Fulham Road after three?' There was the whole of tomorrow to be got through without hope of finding out about Chapman's piano.

'All right,' he said.

'He's torn the skin, look, on his leg, and his knuckle.'

'Can you really hope, or even want, a human-being (if I can call him such for the moment) to go through life without a scratch? Is that your aim? Is that what you really want for him? Not to aim at anything, but to be saved from ever feeling that he's alive? Because that's what you're doing. You're turning him into a vegetable.'

'Yes, I suppose that's what I do try to do,' she admitted, 'not the vegetable I mean, of course not, but the stopping of him ever having to feel pain.' She spoke gently, surmisingly, but added, suddenly roused by her own thoughts, 'Because I don't see the point of pain. Of hurting him. Anyone. It's pointless. It doesn't mean anything. Except pain.'

'I try to wake him up,' he said gently, discussing not arguing, 'I try to turn him into a full human creature, but you pull against me all the time. You keep him dormant, you try to stop him being alive.'

'No, I'm trying to stop him having the worst parts of being alive.'

'And look at the result? He's a half-being! And you're even

69

admitting that you're doing it on purpose, because that's how you want him.'

He had succeeded in frightening her he saw. 'I was hoping to take you to the Coronet tonight,' he said lovingly sulky.

There was only a second's pause during which he saw the misery clearly mark her whole aspect, then she replied, flat-voiced, 'Oh Ed, how lovely, that's lovely – what's on then?'

She would pretend it was a great treat, and in fact she did enjoy films, especially the old select ones that the little cinema in Notting Hill Gate showed; but she could not sit happily through the evening, because going out meant that they had to leave the boy alone. Not that she believed any harm would come to him, what she visualised rather (she had admitted it once) was that he would wake and find himself alone, and panic.

Time had no meaning for him. 'We'll be back soon' didn't register. Ed had told her it was kinder not to tell him they'd be out; he slept deeply, it was highly improbable that he would wake; but if he thought they were out, he might. She agreed, but couldn't reconcile herself to the unspoken deception. She had sat through old Marx Brothers and Garbo films, *Charlie Bubbles*, a James Stewart thriller, and *Easy Rider*, all with the enjoyment spoilt by visualising her waking panicked son. Her mind's eye had taken him downstairs into the icy night and under the wheels of a huge lorry, had left him dead in the road, uncared for.

'Why do you put a whole world of anxiety into one crea-ture?' he had asked. 'Each of us is only ONE. One! Amid countless!'

'Because it's only one each,' she had replied, with certainty. He had not before realised that she had a philosophy; and had been surprised that this central idea of once only was in fact what he was searching for in sound. But for him the once only was the aim, for her it was a condition of existence which she attempted to reconcile herself to.

'Imagine a body,' he said, 'your own, with innumerable corpuscles – and what you're doing is to care for one. One. Doesn't that strike you as ludicrous?'

'When you do first-aid,' she said. . . .

'First-aid! What has that got to do with it . . . ?'

'In first-aid you learn that one ill corpuscle can upset a whole body. . . .'

'So if you don't namby-pander your son, the world will go wrong?'

'Yes, in a way. *My* world anyway. And anyway, you and he are what's near. I can't go and look after a Chinese corpuscle.' She giggled . . . Ed grinned. He adored the self-mockery she was capable of.

'So you just happen to like me because I'm near?' he said, but this time in a bantering tone, as in the old days, before the lump came between them.

'You just go away and see,' she said.

'O.k.' He pressed her against the peeling wall, as he had that prostitute in an alley one raining night. He fingered under her skirt, gently, remembering the rain as the room-tap dripped. His mouth was open, his head pressing hers hard against the wall, feeling the surge of imperativeness as her finger found the opening between the flies, drew back and forth in the slit, before employing the thumb to unbutton and release.

'I wasn't prepared,' she said later.

'You use the pill, don't you?'

'No.'

'Why not?'

'I stopped.'

'Stopped what?'

'Using it.'

'Then you're an idiot.'

'People say it does things to you. You can get hairier and hairier, like an animal, all over. One girl got acne. All over too. Or you can get fat.'

'All right then,' he said, 'you can have another moron instead.'

'Don't, Ed.'

It was evident to her that, subtly, from the day the piano arrived, Ed and Tony were forming a bond from which she was excluded. At first she was relieved, gratified, then immensely happy that Ed should have quite genuinely found a love for the boy he had hitherto despised, and blamed her for. Now, as the boy responded to him (because Ed was now the coaxer, not the punisher), it seemed that he was *his* son, not hers, and that she was, even from Tony's point of view, becoming redundant. And in consequence she was amazed at what strides of confidence and ability Tony made. Could she, she asked herself, ask any more of providence, than that it should make her boy normal? The miracle she had longed for, and even prayed for (though this weakness she hid from Ed who would think it superstitious, old-fashioned and unrealistic) had come to pass, and left her with a feeling, not of sorrow, but of emptiness. Did I really put my need to help him before his need to be helped? she asked herself, and in all honesty answered herself that she really didn't think so – it was just so cold being out of a relationship, the third, the unnecessary. They worked, the two of them, while she shut herself off in the bedroom, listening, pretending to do some chore like darning (she needn't have pretended, they didn't ask what she did), trying to understand, and at first ready to interfere should Tony sob – but later accepting that it was no longer master and pupil, but a duo of creation. In one part of her she questioned whether this extraordinary game they played could be thought of as important work, but another side of her recognised that she was no judge. If I'd been married to Van Gogh I'd have thought his slapping on of paint childish and bad.

At Christmas, Chapman said, some people were going to devise some sort of revue at the Church hall – local talent . . . she mentioned it to Ed just to have something to say that evening. It never entered her head that . . . when she realised how he was taking it she felt her flesh tremble. Then her knees shook. He wouldn't dare make an ass of himself in public, would he? She was panic-stricken. If Ed were laughed at in public he'd never forgive her . . . for having heard of the show from Chapman . . . or for having told him. In truth he'd never forgive himself, which was worse. And what of Tony? She didn't want him whispered about and pitied. She prayed again (praying now being more important to her as she was the more excluded from Ed and the boy) that the committee, or whoever it was that chose the talent, would say 'no' at once to Ed and not be overruled by his insistence. In the meantime, and long before anything was known of who was to do the selecting, Ed had started thinking about clothes and presentation. Tony should have a black suit, white tie, and black-rimmed glasses. She was to look for suitable clothes in the Chapman hiring section, and take him to the optician to have his glasses put into heavy black rims. She felt sick. She couldn't distinguish whether it was a spiritual unease or a physical pain. It enveloped her. She looked in the mirror often now to appal herself with the age she saw in her face, 'like a woman over fifty and I'm only thirty-one'.

She lay between them in bed with the words 'I'm getting between them' unspoken, yet reiterated verbally in her head. 'I'm getting between them.' 'I'm lying between them.'

Ed came to the shop, startled her, it was somehow wrong, cheating, for one of them to visit the other in work-hours.

'Show me the costumes for hire,' he said. There was nothing there for Tony, so he went to a post office and looked up 'theatrical costumiers' in the classified directory, and took a Tube to Leicester Square.

'They've got what I want.'

'Who have?'

'Berman's.'

'What is it?'

'Suit for Tony.'

'And you?'

'I shall go as I am.' He watched her reaction; guarded surprise and disbelief. But he'd meant it. He would dress as inconspicuously as possible: shirt, sleeveless pullover, crumpled grey trousers. He had toyed with the idea of his waiter's coat, but dismissed it as incongruous.

'Nude of course would be better,' he said, not this time to shock her but because nudity in himself with the boy overdressed would have some meaning. 'But in this district they'd never stomach it.'

'Not in any,' she said.

'You don't know. You've never been to the West End.'

'I have!'

'Not in the last five years.'

He had seen posters in which the show advertised displayed nudes. He himself was at first jolted by the male nudes so aggressively photographed, but had quickly restrained his surprise, in return for wanting to be part of this new attitude.

'Where's Tony's clothes then?'

'I told you. Berman's.'

'Didn't you bring them?'

'When you hire,' he explained, 'you do it by the day; so you won't see them till the day of the concert.'

'Suppose they don't fit?'

'Then you'll have to get needle and cotton to them.'

He had had a talk with Chapman while he was looking in the hiring department. Chapman had said he would introduce him to the woman who was running the show. He was glad it was a woman. More chance of selling the act to her – a boy in evening dress would appeal to the females; they'd miss the point of course, but that didn't matter; he didn't expect to be understood.

Tony's response to him had been subtly engineered by Ed in the days after the piano arrived. He saw at once that Tony's thirst for the instrument was not really based on the bangings he had achieved in the shop. What Tony wanted was to be taught, musically, what noise each note or combination of notes would bring forth; and to serve his own ends, Ed was obliged to think up something which would suit them both. Relating his own deeper feelings about destruction to his recognition that if things did not exist they could not be destroyed, and further, that if pure pattern did not exist, there would be no desire for chaos, he finally chose the simple pieces of Bach, written for Anna Magdalena as likely to appeal to Tony and as perfect musically to counterbalance his own destructivity.

He was not wrong in his estimation of his son. No sooner had Ed helped the hard dry little fingers to the first necessary notes, than Tony responded with a love and a demand for more and more that were all he could wish.

He left the boy undisturbed for a few weeks, teaching him to perfect rhythmically three or four of the short pieces; then one evening, he added, about a quarter way through the second piece, a part-destruction; that is, instead of annihilating the boy's sound with his own, he attempted only to mingle it, as perhaps a warning of what was to come. To his amazement the boy seemed not to have heard; was absorbed in the delicate measure he himself was performing. Encouraged, the next night Ed built a heavier edifice, shattered the Bach sound with more force. Tony noticed, but setting his shoulders firmly, carried on with his piece. On the third night Ed knocked down his building with brutal force at the moment he judged most likely to disturb as the coda began to move towards completion. Tony ignored it. For the next two weeks Ed practised interfering, annihilating, at different moments, determined to find the most sensitive spot. If he crashed down near the beginning Tony was indeed perturbed, and would start again before Ed had time to rebuild an edifice, which countered what he was trying to achieve. He finally, late one night, found the balance he wanted: Tony played the first piece without interruption (this was necessary, how otherwise could one indicate the past?). And three-quarters through the second piece, at his most absorbed moment, Ed struck. The result was as he wanted: Tony revolted. Screamed. Buried his head on his arms on the keys, sobbing. All that was necessary now was to teach him to bow to an audience at the end of the first piece. To complete the illusion of the past, of civilities, of the expected. No more practising of the destruction or he might remember; he could, however, go on practising Bach to his heart's delight, and, Ed realised, hers. What a surprise she was in for. She'd think it was all a mistake. So, he supposed, would most of the audience. Good. This way their reaction would be as spontaneous as he desired. Outrage? Compassion? Surprise? Indifference? Demanding their money back? What did it matter? He had a gleeful vision of the organisers coming on stage to apologise. But there were many weeks to go before the show; and Eva could now instruct Tony in perfecting the Bach. She was surprisingly good at it . . . couldn't play herself, but had a perfect ear for rhythm, tone, purity . . . all right, so he'd let her have the boy's attention for the few weeks. The amateur evening would be indicative of what was to come professionally – if. . . .

Ed had no idea how to get the attention of any musician or agent. He browsed in newsagents, reading advertisements at the back of theatrical and erotica magazines. . . . One day he found *The Stage*, the back page of which advertised a list of agents. He bought a copy and took it with him to the post office's classified directory, and copied out the addresses of the most likely-sounding agents. Then he bought *Music and*

Musicians and did the same thing. Next he bought cards. The difficulty was to find someone willing to lend him a typewriter, not that he knew how to type, but he imagined if he pushed the keys, he'd find out fairly quickly how it was done. His boss, a middle-aged Cypriot, had no machine, nor knew of anyone who had. The West Indian family upstairs quite obviously hadn't got such a thing. Eva said Chapman didn't possess one.

'Well, how does he write his business letters then?'

'He doesn't write many.'

'The ones he *does*.'

'He's got headed notepaper E. & R. Penge and he, or sometimes I, just write beneath.'

The possibility came when he met the organiser of the Revue. She was a big heavy-busted determined woman, with glasses, and a strangely beautiful unlined skin. They met at Chapman's, by arrangement, and Ed suggested taking her out for a cup of coffee 'to discuss things'. Eva, of course, couldn't come, she was on duty in the shop. Chapman wasn't asked. Ed took Mrs Hawson (he imagined it was spelt Whoreson and was surprised later when he read her name on the programme) to a tea-room he had never before been to, but he couldn't take her to his own café, and at the one next door there were only stools, and Ed judged his companion to be too grand as well as too wide to enjoy sitting up at a bar.

She told him about the talent she had so far collected, and explained that she had a woman director 'a friend of mine' who would rehearse the items separately, and during the last week or two arrange them in the best order possible, and also perhaps link them with some chosen recorded music, according to the mood of each.

'We've got a superb little troupe of children who do a dance routine,' she said. 'Mrs Latimer taught them for a show last year, not at this hall of course, but they are local children and she can easily get them together again. There's a magnificent baritone, a Mr Selmer, and I've had three or four young persons apply wanting to give a piano recital. Two of them are quite good, and I shall be deciding which one to have very soon. We don't want to double up. . . .' As Ed said nothing she went on 'I gather from Mr Chapman that your little boy plays the piano.'

'Well no,' said Ed, 'not exactly. I mean he does play, yes. Bach.' She raised her eyebrows. 'But it's only part of the act. The whole thing is a Destructo-Symphonia' (that'll catch her, he thought) 'and original in conception.'

'It sounds very intriguing,' she said, 'I'd love to give him an audition.' Ed hesitated. He had absolutely no intention of letting Tony play to anyone but his mother and father before 'the night', because the panic induced when he saw an audience might have wildly unexpected results, which Ed was not prepared to forewarn him of.

'Yes, of course,' he replied, and realised how easy it would be to say 'He's got a cold' when the day or days for the audition came. 'You don't have a typewriter by the way that I could borrow?'

'We can get anything typed you like, if it's invitations or anything like that?'

'Yes,' he said, 'as a matter of fact it is. I have a few professional agents already interested in the boy, and they've asked me to let them know where they can hear him in public.'

From that moment he felt Mrs Whoreson warm towards him. She became positively friendly, elevated him in her conversation to her own level, laughed with him, squeezed his hand at one moment (she was wearing a grey cloth glove, and the touch was by no means exciting to him) and talked of introducing him and the boy to her friend the director.

'I think you'll see,' he ventured, 'when we give the audition, that we won't need rehearsing with anyone else. . . .'

'Just overseeing, shall we call it?'

'He's such a nervous kid, very highly-strung, I don't want to get him worried too soon. Or over-rehearsed, you know.'

'Just overseen,' she insisted.

Ed squeezed the gloved fist. 'Anything you say,' he said gently, and half closed his eyes at her.

'There's a professional conjuror,' she said, her smooth skin suffused now with a deep blush, 'awfully good. And the best of all, which we're keeping till the last item, is a group of four young men who do a *very* funny recitation called "Santa Claus". They've got the costumes, of course, and we're going to fill sacks for them. Such fun.'

'I think we ought to be on near the beginning,' said Ed, visualising ten or eleven agents getting up to leave long before the last item.

'We'll open with the children's troupe,' she said. 'We've promised them.'

'Excellent,' said Ed. 'Then we can come second.'

'We'll see,' she said.

He squeezed the glove again.

Eva was deeply, miraculously, happy. The pain had not recurred ('must have been just depression'), Tony was happy, working with her, responsive, 'ordinary', like an imagined child might be. Ed was in good humour. She sang on her way to school and to work, noticed the trees, the orangeness of the leaves, reflections in puddles, all with a gratitude that they were there, and that she was there to see them. She noticed texture; Tony's hand, the plastic of her handbag, the sheets; she stood at the door of the shop, not as happy now among the antiques as in what was happening on the pavement outside. She told Ed about her happiness. 'I feel like I'm seeing things for the first time.'

He smiled. 'You're looking good too,' he said. Her skin had regained a bloom, her hair a shine, she reminded him now of the lovely girl he'd first met. Recently she'd turned into a drab; no eye for colour, no pride in appearance; an everyday woman, boring. His compliment added to her happiness. She was reminded of what she had been, and of how lately she'd been failing him. She went happily with him to the cinema, even suggesting it herself; realising that now she could communicate with Tony.

'Sleep well; we're going out for a bit. Good boy. We'll be back soon.' He didn't seem to mind. One night, in fact, he crept out of bed when they had gone and started playing, quickly, the Bach. They could hear from the pavement.

'Well I'm damned,' said Ed. They grinned, both satisfied. That evening, during the film, she interlaced her fingers with his, she was relaxed, happy.

As the date, now decided on for 17th December, approached, he got messages through Eva that Mrs Whoreson must see him urgently. When he finally decided to meet her, and face her with the fact that he was not prepared to rehearse, he found her coldly angry.

'I'm afraid we can't include you in the programme,' she said. 'It's a great pity, but I can't take a chance like that. I'm responsible. The programme goes to press tomorrow, and unless you can bring the boy tonight I shall take your act off it.'

'I'll bring him tonight,' said Ed, 'but he's got a slight chill.'

'Wrap him up warm and we won't keep him long,' she replied, her lips pursed.

'I've had three acceptances from agents,' he said in an off-hand manner, and threw in to make it sound more authentic, 'and two more who say they can't attend themselves, but will send representatives.' She was evidently extraordinarily surprised. He felt her change tack, though she said nothing. It would be easy to tell her later that Tony had had a bout of bronchitis and the doctor wouldn't let him out. The programmes, he felt now, would go to press with their name on. II. DESTRUCTO–SYMPHONIA – *Polak and son*. He had thought that intriguing and original.

The extraordinary thing was that Tony did have a fever that night, and a cough, and was flushed and hot.

'He's got to go to a rehearsal,' he told Eva.

'He *can't*,' she said, 'he's ill. He'd catch his death.'

'Well, don't blame me if they won't have us in the programme then.'

'Oh, Ed, see sense.'

He happily played against her maternal care, relishing that it served his purpose, and he was not to blame.

'Well then, *you* tell her.'

'We don't know where she lives.'

'I've got her phone number; you can phone from the Green, but you'll have to be quick or she'll be at the hall waiting for us.'

Eva rushed out.

'He's got a high temperature . . . I'm so sorry . . . I couldn't possibly let my husband bring him. . . .'

'I warned your husband that if he couldn't rehearse we couldn't guarantee that he could appear on the night.'

'I do understand . . . of course . . . you're quite right. They'll be so upset, but it can't be helped.'

'Oh, well. I'll see what we can do.'

'She'll see what she can do.'

'That's o.k. then, well done.'

It was marvellous being praised by him, being on the same side, not pulling against him.

Ed began to get highly excited. All day at the café he planned, re-planned, and as he called it de-planned what would happen. The 'set piece' would be the building of the bric-à-brac (he had collected many more items now) in what order he would not determine until the mood took him on the actual stage. This build-up would take no more than 90 seconds. He always worked fast, neatly, did not pause for thought or re-arrangement; once he had begun the thing took its own course. Then, at the given signal, which he had not yet decided on, but might be the striking of a match, or the shining of a torch (he would tell Tony which just before their act),

Tony would enter, bow, sit at the piano and begin. Ed had rehearsed the bow already; and later the entrance with delightful results: Tony had come into the room, as beckoned, and to Ed's surprise had bowed to the piano. Would he remember that?

In any case to rehearse it again might kill the possibility of his doing it again. Have to chance to luck.

He came back one early evening with the parcel, and told Eva to dress him up. He looked ridiculous enough; enough anyway for Eva to say, 'Oh, doesn't he look sweet!' simply because the jacket was too large for him. Tony fought to get it off until she pinned up the sleeves which left his hands free to play. He looked a little less ridiculous then, though the wide shoulder-padding was ludicrous, and the tails gave him the look of a penguin.

'Where are the black rims to his specs?'

'I tried them, they were too heavy for him.'

'Put them on him.'

'I haven't had his glasses put in them because they were too heavy for him. Just the frames they are. He won't be able to see through them properly I mean. There's no glass.'

'Let's see them.' She reluctantly fetched them.

'No, they're not uncomfortably heavy,' said Ed, 'what he doesn't like is not being able to see, that's all. You take them to the optician's tomorrow, no, on second thoughts I will.' He reached out his hands and took the frames from the boy's face, who was gritching irritably. Eva immediately put back the ordinary glasses with their light-weight childish rims.

'I wouldn't risk it,' she said, 'if he doesn't like them and takes them off he won't be able to see.'

'Then we'll have them put back again.'

'Oh, Ed . . . and what'll he do without his own glasses if you take them with you?'

'It's Saturday tomorrow – no school.'

'He'll hate it.'

'He won't. He'll practise. He doesn't read music anyway.'

On the seventeenth Ed arrived at two-thirty as arranged, at the hall. Mrs Whoreson was seated in the stalls with the director and a few scattered mothers of the children's troupe. The troupe had apparently been through their routine, and were standing waiting for comment on the stage, while Mrs Whoreson and the director conferred.

'Oh good, you're in time,' she said to Ed. The house lights were on, and only a working-light on the stage. Ed came and pushed down the seat next to her.

After polite exchanges he said, 'What sort of lighting will I be having?'

Mrs Whoreson called out: 'All right children. Thank you. That'll do. Good luck for tonight.'

The director added, 'Sheila, don't forget your pumps, dear, you can't dance in gym shoes; and, Carol, will you ask your mother to take the ribbon off your hair, dear, because it makes your head out of time with the others. All right, dismiss.'

'The piano ought to be on the stage while they're dancing,' Ed said, 'and just be shoved into place when the curtain comes down.'

'No, it can't be,' said the director, 'the children use the whole stage. It's in the wings. We'll have Ernie to push it on.'

'Is he here now?'

'No, not till six o'clock.'

'Oh, then we can't rehearse.' Ed saw the opportunity for making it their fault and not his.

'Where's your boy? I want to see what he's wearing.'

'He'll be along,' said Ed, 'I'll try out the piano.' And he went quickly towards the pass-door on to the stage, past children in tartan tutus coming down the steps into the auditorium to reclaim their mothers, and be praised. To his surprise the piano was a baby-grand. Just what Tony had been used to. He ran his fingers professionally over the notes, partly to see if they all played (to his delight three or four did not) and partly to impress the two women that he really was a professional musician whom they were lucky enough to have appearing in their amateur show. 'There are notes missing!' he called out angrily, as if this would never do.

'Oh dear,' she called back.

'You'll have to get someone to it,' he yelled, his voice travelling round the proscenium arch as if it were shut up in a box.

'We can't. It's Sunday.'

'God damn it!' he said, and strode across the stage as if he would walk off and might not appear that evening.

'You should have come to rehearsals,' she countered, yelling too.

He stopped mid-stage and looked contrite.

'I'll have to go and warn him,' he said.

'Yes, of course.' Her voice was low now too, admitting that he was not altogether to blame.

'Is Mr Selmer here?'

'Bin here an hour,' was muttered from the back of the stalls.

Selmer was already in full evening dress, would have spoilt Tony's effect, Ed thought, but that luckily Tony would be on first. Might even get an unlooked-for laugh for Mr Selmer's appearance, following Tony's.

'Excuse me,' Ed bowed, and left, before there could be any more decisions, about what time Tony would have to be there, or whether he should be inspected first. The piano in fact was just what he wanted, and with Ernie's help could be moved into position in a few seconds. Bad to keep an audience waiting after the number one act; good if they had just time to say wasn't that nice to each other, clap, and resettle themselves. He had had no reply from any of the typed invitations sent out, but he still had a hope that perhaps someone would turn up, and he planned to take Tony to the front of house foyer at the end of the act, to meet them, leaving Eva at the stage door in case that was where they expected a rendezvous.

The show was due to start at seven-thirty. Ed planned to arrive with Eva and the boy just after the curtain went up on the children's troupe. This would leave just enough time for Mrs W to panic, and Tony to be utterly bewildered. He would tell them at home that it started at eight, and suddenly spring on them that they were next. If Mrs W appeared backstage to interfere and fuss so much the better. He could trust Eva to stand at the side of the stage and push Tony on at the given signal. What should it be? On the way home he decided upon a word signal 'Now!' that would be appropriate enough, short, and he hoped would hold the audience's attention. If Tony took his time after that, so much the better.

'When I say "now",' he said to Eva, 'keep him back for a count of five, and then tell him to come on and bow. Don't rehearse it,' he insisted, 'or you'll spoil it.'

'But suppose he won't come on?'

'Don't *fuss*. I'll come and fetch him.'

'O.k. then.' She seemed satisfied. 'I wish I could watch him ... you ... from the front.'

He explained about the pass-door. She had put green mascara on her eyelids.

'Where did you get that?'

'At the chemist's?' the question in her voice was underlyingly attached to the unspoken, 'Why, don't you like it?' Ed smiled.

It suited her, and she'd evidently put her hair in curlers and then back-combed it. He'd never understood her, why did she assume that wearing green eye-shadow in the wings would add something to the performance?

'It's very nice,' he said, and kissed her. Tony was wearing the heavy-rimmed glasses already, though irritably; but he felt lost when he couldn't see, except when his hand was in hers, or on the notes.

'Tony looks good too. We don't have to be there till seven-thirty. We're not on till eight,' he said, keeping concealed the typed programme in his pocket, 'so he needn't dress up for hours yet, and he can take the glasses off if he wants to.'

'No,' said Tony, and shoved at them with his hand. 'No.'

'He ought to practise in the jacket, he hasn't done yet,' she said, and opened the lid of the piano. Ed banged it shut, startling her. 'No practising.'

Tony puckered up his face, the prelude to the usual roar of refusal to comply, the blood rushing with temper to his neck, face, and more predominantly his ears. Ed sat on the chair and pulled him towards him.

'Got a new piano for you,' he said.

'No, no, no,' said the boy automatically as always at any sign of explanation or talk from his parents; but the blood calmed, and he was evidently listening, half-believing, but not accustomed to give way.

'No!' he shouted in his father's face, but did not pull away.

'Very soon – this evening. We're all going out together and I'll show you the new piano and you can play it. I'll be there with you. And your mother.' Eva had been shocked to hear Ed pretending that the new piano would be his, but the admission that she would be with Tony stopped her from remonstrating. She sided with Ed when Tony pulled away from him and opened the piano lid.

'No, not now,' she said; but understanding him better than his father, she added, 'This one's still yours, you can come back to it. You'll see it again tonight. After playing the other one.'

'As if he could follow all that rigmarole,' said Ed. But Tony was evidently pacified, and Ed took him on his knee, a rare occurrence, and sang 'Willikins and His Dinah' to him, with Eva grinning beside them. This was family life, she thought; and worth being late getting ready and having to rush. She had been going to put on the false eye-lashes she'd treated herself to, she'd practised them and they weren't too bad, but she'd have to forgo that now if she was to be ready in time. She put on her best dress, redid her hair, took Tony to the

86

lavatory three times although he didn't need it, and went herself twice, out of excitement.

'We'll take a taxi,' said Ed, 'if we can find one.' She
laughed with excitement and the newness of it all. He went
downstairs at twenty past seven and hailed one. Tony sat
rigid all senses cocked, taking in the lights, the darkness,
the sensation of being in a car, the feeling of approbation
of the parents on either side of him.

'Bit further on, on the left.' The hall was undistinguished
but lit up – cars were parked all along the pavement and up
the side street. From the sound he thought he gathered the
children's troupe were nearing the finish of their bit. Mrs W
would be in a tizz, hastily getting number three to come on
as number two, rehearsing what she'd say to the audience,
hating him for disrupting her great night. He paid the taxi,
and with speed, shepherded them to the side door, which led
on to the stage.

'Listen,' said Eva, hurrying a bit breathless, beside him,
'they've begun! And it's only just after half past seven!' He
didn't answer, ran quickly, followed by her and the boy to the
side wings; nodded to Mrs W in the dark.

'Oh, *there* you are,' she said, very angrily, 'you've
practically wrecked the whole evening!'

'Disgraceful,' added the director, and while she went on
muttering at him, he verified that his apparatus was where he'd
left it, ready to be moved on from the left.

'I hope the stage hand's here,' he said, 'Ernie or whatever
his name is.'

'No,' she admitted, deflated, 'he can't come.'

'Fuck!' said Ed, which successfully shut her up. He'd have to
bring on his own stuff, build, then push on the piano by himself, he supposed. Bad arrangement; the audience would have
time to cough, and think he was wasting time. He saw Selmer.

'Give me a hand, Mr Selmer,' he asked gently, 'I've been
let down by the stage hand.'

'Anything of course . . .' said Mr Selmer.

The children's troupe took their bow, the curtain came down, a shrill outburst of chatter overlaid the parental applause.

'Just push the piano on from the other side for me, will you, when I give you the cue. Can't do it myself, I shall be on stage.' Mr Selmer raised his eyebrows.

'Isn't there anyone else . . .' he began.

'Shut up!' yelled Ed at the children, 'and for Christ's sake get to your seats without noise, the next act's on.' They hurried, subdued, through the pass-door to join their mummies and daddies; 'When do you want curtain up, sir, the director seems to have walked out?' a man said patiently.

'Put it up now, then walk across stage and give a hand with the piano to Mr Selmer,' said Ed authoritatively.

'What me! Walk on stage with the curtain up! Not likely!' But he pressed the button for 'curtain up' at once, and left them to it. Ed saw an opportunity, as through the door to the stage came a Father Christmas. . . .

'Excuse me,' he said quickly, 'I'm on. Before they put the curtain up could you go across the stage and help Mr Selmer move the piano.'

'Rightie-ho!' said the man, pushing back his hood, and revealing a very young face under the white cotton-wool beard. He walked across the stage and the audience 'Ah'd' with appreciation, some laughed, some clapped; Father Christmas gave an agonised look towards the auditorium, said 'Jesus!' too loudly, and scuttled off to join Mr Selmer. Ed in the meantime came on stage and was quickly piling the bicycle wheel on to the table, the ladder, the bell . . . the rest of the apparatus. He could see Tony's glasses glinting in the wings.

'Not yet,' he said, 'good boy. Come on,' he called impatiently over to the other side of the stage. The audience's bewilderment and discomforture started as Mr Selmer who was known to some of them, and the half Father Christmas pushed the piano in front of them, and retired as quickly as they could. Ed was ready. He stood centre stage and struck a match. Tony failed to enter.

'That's his cue,' he called irritably to Eva. Tony, after the preliminary push, shuffled unhappily towards his father. The audience, delighted, called out an 'Ah!' of appreciative compassion.

'Bow!' hissed his father. Tony clutched his flies.

'Pi-pi,' he said.

'Piano first, pi-pi after,' said Ed loudly. There was a hush in the hall, then the noise of a seat going up, then another. 'That'll be Mrs W and friend,' he thought. Tony miraculously went towards the new piano and bowed at it twice, the audience were reassured, they 'Ah'd' again, starting chattering. The boy perched himself on the stool, either deaf to them, or too concentrated to bother. Certainly, as far as he was concerned, the people in the next room had nothing to do with him. He started to play, the chattering stopped. Ed was as happy as he could have hoped. It was all perfect. He waited till the second piece was well under way, then he reached up and pushed the top article of his edifice. He had to push three times before the thing tumbled completely, but managed to keep the noise continuous and was gratifyingly aware of the roar of orgasmic incompletion and the total misery of the child who stood yelling, wetting his Berman-hired pants and flinging his glasses on to the floor.

Tony now plonked himself hard on to his bottom, shooting his legs out wide, his body bent over between them so that the roar of pain and despair fell with his forehead on to the floor-boards. He kept up the enclosed roar not noticing the disturbance in the audience, the shouts of dismay as the director and Mrs Hawson attempted to get on to the stage from the auditorium. Eva had darted up the steps to the pass-door, having only a few moments before come down them to witness The Scene. She was now trying vainly to pull Tony to his feet by an arm, to gather him to her, to comfort him. He was as rigidly immovable, as unaware of her efforts as of the world around him. After a few seconds she slipped to the floor beside him, hugging him, trying to find his face to kiss, his eyes to wipe, his ear to comfort.

'It's all right, darling,' she kept saying, as she usually did when things were at their worst. Ed smiled, his heart was high with pleasure, but he knew it would be prudent to leave before the viragos attacked him. He slipped into the wings, and quickly out of the stage-door, mentally making a note that he would fetch his belongings tomorrow. Eva and Tony would not suffer by his absence – they would be cosseted not abused by the viragos. Humming under his breath with achieved delight, he walked briskly along the dimly-lit pavement – his footsteps sharp and decisive, clear in the night air.

He was already nearing the Bush when he remembered. The agent! Or agents! Was he (Ed thought of him as the one perspicacious one among others who may have turned up) waiting in the foyer – or had he come backstage to see him? If so Eva's attitude would put him off. She would be certain it was all a terrible unmentionable mistake. He cursed himself for being an idiot to miss the main chance, having so carefully planned for it, but was already composing a letter – he still had those addresses – 'I have been informed that a musical or theatrical agent was asking for me after Polak and son last night – but as no one can tell me what name or address, I am writing to enquire whether by chance it was yourself. . . .'

That sort of thing to all of them; then if no one was in fact there, it might awaken an interest . . . just because he said 'someone' was interested. This he told himself was how interest grew into compound interest. First get the ball rolling. He made an over-arm gesture . . . and crossed the road. He was still in a state of excitement when he got in – but there was nothing to do as he'd left all his apparatus at the hall. He undressed, lit a cigarette and got into bed to review, lying down, the evening's events. Two or three times he laughed aloud at his memories . . . but always in front of his mental eye was the picture of Eva distraught, gathering the boy to her.

'I'll have to tell her,' he thought, 'she'll never get there on her own.'

He sat up in bed as he heard them, ready to defend himself from her expected onslaught. . . . 'How *could* you – in front of all those people – how could you be so *cruel* to him.' Instead they came in quietly, both faces swollen and blotched from crying and temper – hers purple, thickened, almost as ugly as the boy. He saw for the first time the likeness between them, the possibility that the child derived from her. He smiled, waiting. She started undressing Tony in silence, the boy stood eyelids drooping, concentrating only on the need for immediate sleep, possibly, Ed thought, the evening's happenings already forgotten, as the present as usual powerfully took hold of him. She was pulling off his vest over his head, manipulating his sagging arms through the holes, before she spoke.

'He couldn't help it,' she said contritely, '. . . Ed; it was too much for him.' Apologising? Thinking the boy had let him down? He smiled secretly, arranging this mood of hers so that it should fit neatly in between what had happened and what was to come. He said nothing. She carried the naked, dirtied boy and his clothes off to the basin in the other room.

'We'll have to have them cleaned before we send them back to the shop,' she said practically, 'I can't wash them properly I don't think.' He made himself join in this small-talk.

'It'll cost more if we keep them another day.'

'Can't be helped.'

She was contrite. She touched him tentatively with her fingers when she lay beside him in bed; as if asking forgiveness, as if it were her fault. He felt the bed shake with his suppressed laughter, he lay over her so that the shaking came out of his mouth and on to hers. She freed her mouth; whispered aghast, 'You're not crying? Ed?'

'No: laughing,' he whispered back, 'about the only thing I *can* do, isn't it?'

She moaned. 'I've got such a pain,' she said, 'it's agony.'

There'd be no school till after Christmas. Eva had got up alone, brought some tea and bread to Ed.

'Don't wake him, let him sleep on.'

'I've got to go out too. Collect my things.'

'Never mind.'

'I'll be back before I go off to work.'

'Give him some bread then if he wakes.' They were both being solicitous for the boy. Eva gratefully, as though Ed were being magnanimous. He *felt* solicitous. After she'd gone he lay eating, letting the crumbs fall on to the bedclothes; watching that head.

'Give him a holiday from music too,' he thought, 'even if he doesn't want one. Keep him away from the piano until he can bear it no longer. Pity there's no key to it . . . perhaps I can stick the lid down.'

Tony woke while he was pulling on his underpants; stared at him without seeing; the blank-eyed obstinate look.

'Good boy,' said Ed, 'you were a very good boy last night.' He came and sat on the bed by him, pulling on his thick pull-over, the look of the icy sky out of the window making him feel chilled.

'Very good,' he added, as his head emerged through the narrow neck-hole. 'You want some bread?'

'Yes.'

'Milk?'

Tony shook his head. Ed remembered his own irritation at

Eva for 'waiting on' the child – 'can't he get a bit of bread for himself for Christ's sake . . .' but he needed to coddle him now, felt himself drawn to the boy, accepting of his thick backwardness, even fearful that it might disappear and leave him with an ordinary child.

'Won't be long.'

He brought a hunk of bread and gave it to the boy while he pulled on his socks and shoes.

'Cold out,' he said conversationally. 'I'm off to get the apparatus – but I'll be back before I go to work. No school today, eh? Holidays!' Tony smiled at him; a broad childish grin that rammed into his heart. It was as if a dog had spoken; had fooled one for years that it was dumb and had suddenly said, without realising it had spoken, 'Let's go for a walk, shall we?' He tousled the hair with his hand.

'Good boy,' he repeated, 'you stay there. Won't be long.' It was as if he had a new element to cope with. He felt self-conscious, wondered whether he was up to it, but elated, excited. Alive.

He cared little whom he met at the hall, should there be anyone there at ten in the morning. He hoped a caretaker, or a sweeper-up of sorts. But should it be a whole pack of viragos he was ready for them; impregnable. He had his tape with him; whistled a tune for it, muffled in his pocket, held it to his mouth now and then for a sharpener; offered it to rumbling wheels, his and other footsteps, snatches of passing words. It was as he expected an icy day, the sounds were crisp, staccato, they didn't linger on the air as summer lazy sounds, but cut themselves off briskly, contracting.

The hall was locked. Padlocked. He limped round it looking for entry. No good climbing in one of those small windows; he'd never get the stuff out through it. A red-faced man in a cloth cap came up the path. They glared at each other.

'I left my stuff here last night,' Ed said, 'have you got the keys?' The cold man put his hand in his pocket, undecided.

'What stuff?'

'Music stuff. In the wings, at the side of the stage.'

'All right then.'

'I'll get a taxi while you open up then.'

The man didn't reply; put a small key in the padlock.

He took twenty minutes to get a taxi; reckoning that the amount of money needed to take his apparatus from home and back was much more than he could reasonably afford. He didn't ask the driver to come in and help, nor would he ask the old doorman; both would expect adequate tipping. He did it himself in three journeys; while the taxi-driver sat elbow propped, resting his cheek on his hand, and the doorman unlocked the stage door cubby-hole and took off his mittens.

Ed had stowed the stuff in the cab and by the driver, and was about to get in when he re-saw what he had barely noticed when it happened – the doorman placing two buff-coloured envelopes and a folded piece of white paper, into the pigeon holes . . . he went back.

'One for me?' he asked casually. 'I'm expecting a message – after the performance last night.' As he spoke, he realised just how low he must be in his own estimation if he had to brag to this poor old geyser; he knew of course that there would be nothing for him, no message of any kind, but he could not refrain from keeping up the pretence to himself that someone might have left him a note.

'What name?' the old man asked suspiciously, holding the note away from Ed's possible sight.

'Polak.'

'No,' said the old man, and started to put it back. . . . 'How do you spell it?'

'P.O.L.A.K.'

'P.O.?'

'L.A.K.' He felt foolish. Nothing had prepared him for the fact that there might in truth be a note for him. He felt queasy; held out his hand.

'Yes,' he said, 'that's it.' He'd have to tip the man now. As he put his hand in his pocket to feel for his change, bad temper seized him. Of course the note would be from that Whore bitch; she'd know he'd be coming back for his stuff. He was immensely angry with himself for the hope he had generated in himself. Aloud he called her three filthy names, whilst the old man picked his teeth with a bitten-off matchstick, so as not to look as if he were waiting for the pocket hand to produce something for him. Ed found 5p, reluctantly, now that he had guessed what he was paying for, and handed it over. 'Bye sir.'

He gave the address and got in the taxi, opened the piece of paper, ready to crumble it and throw it out of the window. 'Phone 437 8914.' His stomach lurched, re-set trembling. He leaned towards the driver about to ask him to stop at the Bush so that he could phone, realised in time that he would already be late for work, added the clause that in any case Mr 437 must be kept waiting a short while not to show an over-eagerness, and sat back with a boy's excitement surging through him. He unpacked his apparatus, tipped the driver well, bounded upstairs with the stuff, and was about to dash off only ten minutes late to the café when he noticed through the open door the boy. He'd forgotten about him.

'Must go, I'm late,' he said, but took the time to bound into the bedroom and kiss him as a child might greet his mother when he had achieved top marks.

'Is this 437 8914?'

'Who's this?'

'I'm not quite sure,' said Ed, 'who I want to speak to. I have a message to phone 437 89 . . .'

'Who's this?' the female voice insisted.

'My name is Polak,' and he added foolishly, 'and son.'

'Who?' said the voice.

'Polak. I've got a message here to phone. . . .'

'Hold on.'

He held on.

After some minutes the racing pulse of the unsatisfied telephone announced that it needed to be fed. He inserted another twopenny bit and waited. One of the two girls in the next kiosk was talking interminably. The other bit at one side of her thumb thoughtfully, as if it were a succulent chicken drumstick. Outside three people had to wait their turn. It was raining. Ed turned his back on them.

'Who's this?' said another voice; this time male.

'My name's Ed Polak. You left a message for me to phone.'

'Reference to what?'

'My son . . . he performed on the piano . . . we did. . . .'

'Oh yes – bring him along at 11.30 tomorrow' and he put the phone down.

'Bring him along where, you silly b . . .' Ed shouted, because no one was on the other end of the line. But he was excited. He had another twopence . . . dialled again, said to the female voice, 'I have an appointment at 11.30 tomorrow – name of Polak – can you give me the exact address?'

'What address?'

'Your address.'

'Oh . . . 137 St Martin's Row.'

She had put the phone down again before he said thank you, so he added 'silly bitch'.

'Done any touring?'

'No.'

'I mean yourself.'

'No.'

'Got a card?'

'No – only . . .'

'Equity?'

96

'No.'

'Naatke?'

'No.'

'Musicians?'

'No.'

Rudge whistled between his teeth.

'Might get away with it on account of his age. Doubt it. In any case he needs piano lessons. The idea's fine, but he's not good enough to destroy. Not yet.'

Ed was amazed that this third-rate long-toothed individual should have probed his own thoughts – got the idea.

'Got any private money?'

'No.'

'No savings?'

'I've got £500 saved up,' Ed admitted. He wasn't going to admit the lot.

Rudge doodled. 'Say three quid a lesson – three's into 500 . . .' he scratched his head, muttered, redid the sum . . . 'makes,' he said, '166 lessons and a bit. At twice a week makes 83 weeks equals a couple of years. We'll probably need a year. You'd have to invest £250 in him. Prepared to do it?'

'Yes,' said Ed. 'But I can teach him myself.'

'Nonsense.' Rudge made a movement with his head as if throwing out both Ed and the idea. He picked up the phone. 'Get me Dolly.' He put the phone down. Immediately it rang again. His hand was still on it. He picked it up. 'Yes?' Crackle . . . voice, crackle . . . voice, 'put him on. Yes, Ted.' He started doodling again, listening. Picked a tooth. Changed ears.

The call lasted three or four minutes. Rudge didn't speak. Finally he said 'Mm. Mm' and put the receiver down. The phone rang again at once. 'Oh, good, put her on. Dolly? How're you love? Not so bad, not so bad.' (Weather, laugh, flirt, money et cetera – why didn't the man come to the point?) 'Listen, Dolly, I've got a kid in the office . . . no, five-year-old

G.I.I.—D

. . . moronic, sort of . . . no jokes, but got something musically. Piano. Yes – heard him myself. Badly taught. Want to handle it? I've said three quid a lesson. Super. Right. Father name of Polak.' He turned to Ed. 'What's the boy's name? Tony,' he said into the mouthpiece. 'We'll probably change that. Okay, love, be seeing you.'

'The rest of the money,' he said to Ed, but not looking up, 'might well be invested in taking him to concerts,' he held up a hand to silence what he imagined would be Ed's protest – 'not modern stuff,' he said, 'but good old-fashioned piano-playing. Make him ambitious – make him want to play like the great ones. Has he got an ear?'

'I think so,' said Ed, and Tony, who seemed not to have followed a word since he arrived, put up his hands to his old knitted cap and felt beneath the earpieces. They were both there. He nodded.

'Got ears,' he said distinctly. Both men ignored him.

'You don't have to come,' said Ed.

'No, I'd like to. I'll pay for my ticket.'

'For Christ's sake, can't you think of anything but money?'

He had indeed been annoyed at the thought of having to buy three tickets instead of two every time he'd want to take the boy to a concert – but he parried.

'You don't understand music, it's a waste of time taking you.'

'But I like listening, and I'd like to be with you both.'

'Thought you said you weren't feeling well,' he muttered.

'That was yesterday.'

'Getting tenacious in your old age, aren't you?'

But his irritation subsided when evening came and she looked so young and presentable. He'd wanted to be alone with his son, proud of him at the Festival Hall, but on reflection what was there to be proud of in the appearance of the child? Didn't matter what you did to him, combed his hair, dressed him well, he still looked deprived. Mentally deprived.

Eva dithered, argued with herself. Her wish to go to the concert was countered by her intelligence telling her that Ed would be happier without her, and being happier would be more pleased with his son. If I'm there he'll find fault with Tony, if only to reproach me: if I'm not, he'll overlook little irritations. . . . Yes but oh how exciting, how wonderful, how heartening to be with them both at a concert; and with a purpose; we'll have a right to be there, to listen, to spend the money, to be part of . . . but no, it won't be like that if I'm there, it'll feel anxious, ill-at-ease . . . I can't. . . .

'I don't really think I will come, after all,' she said.

'Why not?'

'I don't feel . . .'

'Don't say you don't feel well; you haven't looked so good for months . . . don't funk it now.'

'I've got that pain again . . .'

She hadn't but it was the only excuse. And yet now he was arguing for her to go, she wasn't sure whether he would genuinely like her to, or was playing the game because he was now safe in the knowledge that she wasn't coming.

She beamed suddenly. Why should she deprive herself of such a huge pleasure when perhaps he really would be pleased if she went. 'O.k. I'll come,' she said.

'Don't come for me.'

'No. I'd love to. The pain's very slight.'

'Make up your *mind*,' he muttered.

No, he had just been playing, he hadn't really wanted her – she realised now.

'I won't come,' she said.

'For Christ's sake.'

But she saw his shoulders relax with relief; he wouldn't risk another thrust.

But after a few concerts Ed decided that Eva could take the boy. He was willing to pay out, he said, as long as he didn't have to sit through all that stuff. Yes, it was 'great art' he said, yes it was all that it was cracked up to be, but it wasn't for him. What mattered to him was the sound of sound, not the sound of art. His one desire as he listened to Brendel playing was to throw a dagger at him and listen to the effect on all those nice quiet listeners, who only seemed to come to life between movements when they shuffled, snuffled and coughed at God knows how many decibels. He regretted not having his tape-recorder with him for those moments of release. He was satisfied after two minutes, glancing at Tony, that the child was enraptured. Good. Now Eva could get on with it, and thank him for his kindness into the bargain.

There were concerts, however, that did interest him – not the ones Rudge advised for the boy – but those he wanted to go to for his own sake. Let Eva and Tony get on with the necessary traditional stuff he was training the boy for – he felt justified in spending something on his own enjoyment too. Not that he thought very highly of what he heard, Stockhausen, Cage (he was nearer) . . . but there were pleasurably unforeseeable moments.

There was the concert at the Queen Elizabeth Hall that advertised Stockhausen among others. The first item was ordinary enough: a short uninspired piece for three trombones. One player stood facing inwards as though shielding his instrument from the audience and gradually moved round until first another back and then the other was presented.

The second item on the programme was by Stockhausen. A piano solo. Eight instrumentalists and two sopranos walked on to the platform in a desultory way as if they were taking independent strolls in a park on a hot Sunday. Then a woman from the audience got up and walked to the rostrum, standing in front of and below it. She spoke a few sentences in a huffy, bored, foreign accent and went back to her seat. The dark soprano sang with her back to the audience, far up stage – the fair one sang one note only, which she held for the first few beats of the piece, and then stood silently. There was no pianist.

The audience were clearly puzzled. Where did modern music begin and end? Was this piece really a piano solo? Would they appear foolish to their next-door neighbour if they doubted it? Ed had no such qualms. It was clearly neither solo nor piano. He got out of his seat as the piece ended and the players drifted off, and came down the steps until he reached the row where the woman who had made the opening announce-ment sat.

He got her attention and said, 'What was it you said? We couldn't hear at the back.'

She looked offended. Said something unintelligible which he heard quite clearly but couldn't understand.

'What?' he said.

She repeated slowly, with mock precision, as if he were the foreigner, 'I was saying the tympanist is not the one who was to be playing.'

'Yes,' persisted Ed, 'but it wasn't by any stretch of imagina-tion a piano solo, was it?'

'What?' she asked irritably (the players were coming on stage for the next piece).

'It wasn't a piano solo,' he shouted, banging his forefinger on to his programme, 'by Stockhausen.'

She shrugged. 'He didn't arrive in time from Holland,' she said, as if it were Ed's fault, and turned away. Ed was de-lighted. A stupid woman, spreading confusion in an audience about when-was-a-piano-solo-not-a-piano-solo in this gracious atmosphere of musical *savoir* appealed to him. Destructo, he decided wryly, existed everywhere without the help of his art – but his art, he thought with pride, would point a finger at it, elevate it to a place of recognition. He left the concert hall highly pleased with the evening's entertainment and his own prospects for the future.

Ed treated himself to the pleasure of writing to Mrs Hawson, '. . . Tony now has a professional agent, thanks to his appearance in your amateur evening. . . .' He addressed it to 'Mrs Hawson', but inside wrote 'Dear Mrs Whoreson. . . .'

The house in Shepherd's Bush was being demolished; all the inhabitants would have to find somewhere else to live . . . he had taken time off from his waiter's job . . . Eva had missed some days at the shop when she didn't feel well (he knew it was psychological because she sensed the boy's affection leaving her in favour of his father), and what with the concerts and piano lessons money was getting to be a big problem. No point in going outside London either. The fares and time spent getting into town for lessons with Dolly wouldn't be worth what they might save on the move. He left Eva to look for alternative accommodation; he was too preoccupied.

After a couple of months he went to see Rudge again; took an 88 bus to Charing Cross – give himself time to think; listen to new sounds. He'd do the Underground coming back. Bit obvious that – been done a lot. Menacing. But he might catch something on a bus . . . especially if he sat near the boarding platform. The conductress had a cold, her fingers were bluish, chapped. And there was a dark line either side of her parting where the peroxide had grown out. A heavy woman got into the bus at Notting Hill Gate and pressed herself between him and another man. Her heavy carnation scent invaded him, her hips through the coat pressed against his. She didn't move away when the other fellow got off though there was now room to ease herself. She remained pressed against him, her eyes staring vacantly at the seat opposite.

'What the eye doesn't see the body isn't doing,' Ed said to himself.

He felt he was in bed with her all the way to Piccadilly Circus, half excited, half sick with the smell.

Sitting opposite Rudge in the small overheated office he said, 'I'm spending out, but what's going to happen in a year

. . . will we get a union card? If not, I'm spending out with no hope of return, aren't I?'

Rudge twiddled a biro round and round between his fingers. 'There *is* a way,' he said, 'but we won't be able to do anything about it yet. I'll let you know nearer the time. The year's lessons have barely started.'

'What way?'

'Leave that to me.'

Ed was loath to leave it. What way could there be? Unions were unions and closed shops were closed shops, and Rudge didn't at all look the sort of individual who'd have any power with union officials. In fact, he looked like a man who didn't work, soft, perfumed, old-fashioned, with the nose of a gambler. But with authority. 'Leave it to me,' he said, and Ed could get no further.

'How's he getting on with Dolly?' Having silenced Ed on one point, Rudge was prepared to show interest.

Ed, to his dissatisfaction, had been allowed to attend only the first ten minutes of Tony's first lesson – since then she had firmly closed the door on him as he delivered the boy. The piano behind another shut door was too far away from the hall for him to gain anything by eavesdropping. So he had no idea what went on. Tony, of course, was quite unable to give any indication to his father . . . all he had to judge by was his practising; and melodically he supposed he was making progress – not, he deemed, £6 worth of progress each week, however. But he was caught. If he offended Rudge he would he knew never get another chance of becoming professional. He had lost his independence, not only of choice but of spirit, and it made him sick with a physicality he would not have thought possible to produce from a nervous unease. He kept reminding himself that a year from now, though Rudge might still manage their career (at twelve per cent, the agreed price, 'because he's a child, you know') he and Tony between them would soon rise above and beyond such minimal, but at the moment, indispensable help. 'Once on the ladder,' Ed thought, 'we'll show him who's on which rung.' In the meantime, the effort and patience were turning his stomach sour.

'Passably,' he replied to Rudge's question.

'She's fantastic with children,' Rudge countered, 'and she says he's exceptionally talented.'

Ed looked at his hand, trying to judge whether this was diplomacy. If so, he supposed, it was diplomacy aimed at a twelve per cent of Tony's talent, and if that were the aim, who was he to complain.

'Keep me in touch', said Rudge, and held out his hand. This was his usual way of getting rid of clients and would-be clients. He was always at his most beamingly polite when someone was about to leave the office – like a young child who refuses to talk or go near guests of his parents, but will gleefully and amicably wave goodbye from the window as they depart.

Rudge had not told Dolly of Ed's Destructo music – she would never have accepted to teach him if she had dreamed that it was for the purpose of destroying not only the music, but the child. She was like a gypsy, with her uncombed hair and her swinging gait, and she wore ankle-length cotton print skirts which emphasised the likeness. She was a good teacher, but had a formidable temper, which burst not upon her pupils but upon their parents. If anyone dared so much as to stick up for themselves, she locked herself in a silence whose fury would make her opponent wish they'd not only never met her, but never dreamed of having their child taught the piano.

Rudge had sent young aspirants to her for voice-training in speech and song as well as for piano. Few of the children liked her; but she loved them all. Ed had been warned not to tell her anything of his future plan for Tony.

'He's being taught the piano, full stop,' Rudge had said.

But Ed managed to persuade her not to attempt to teach the boy to read music.

'He couldn't,' he told Dolly in those few moments when he

first met her. 'They can't get him to see words at school. He plays by touch, and ear, that is, his touch and ear memory function, but give him something to do with his eyes, he can't see what's on paper any more than a dog can. To him it's a piece of paper – marked if you like, or grey or whatever . . .'

'Doesn't he see pictures on paper?' Dolly had asked.

'Dogs don't.'

'But does he?'

'Never asked him,' said Ed, 'because he doesn't get on with questions.'

Strangely, although she was a very obstinate creature, she didn't attempt to get him to read music. Ed knew this because when Tony got home he'd go to the piano and place his fingers on notes as firmly and gently as if a woman's hands were on his, guiding them. Ed was pleased. At least the woman wasn't ruining his own work – at £3 a time.

After ten weeks the pieces he was mastering were no longer the ones from the Anna Magdalena notebook, but more complicated, lengthy and, for his small fingers, more difficult technically. Ed was not at first sure that his destruction would have such an effect on these advanced pieces as on Tony's earlier more childish accomplishments, but after consideration he decided it might suit his purposes as well, if not better. After all, he told himself, the higher the accomplishment the further it would have to fall.

'There's a concert,' said Ed, 'called The Society of Prevention of Modern Music. Want to come?'

'Where?' asked Eva. She would parry until she knew if he intended taking Tony.

'Does it matter?'

'Well, I mean,' she said quickly, 'is it a club?'

'No. For the public.'

'The prevention of cruelty to music?' she said, and giggled, the way he liked.

'You would get it wrong. You do think it's cruelty, don't you? What I'm doing? Breaking rules? Establishment norms?'

'Well,' she said, still smiling, 'that's what you called it, isn't it?'

'I did not.'

'Well, what did you?'

'No wonder you misunderstood. You don't listen.'

'But I'm sure you said . . .'

'All right,' he said, 'if you're sure . . .'

'What did you say then?'

He didn't answer.

'Where's it on?'

'Does it matter?'

'Are you taking Tony?'

'Depends.'

'On whether I go?'

He didn't answer, but as usual she carried on working it out to herself . . .

'This could mean he'll take him *if* I go or he'll take him if *I don't*. So I'll say nowt,' she said to herself, surprised at using that particular word to herself.

But as it turned out they all three went, and Ed was in a good mood. It was at the Queen Elizabeth Hall he told her.

'Do you want to go by Tube?'

Eva nudged him, and nodded with her head along past him to his left. She was wearing a knitted cap, not unlike Tony's. He loathed it, decided tonight not to tell her to take it off, and now was quite pleased to find that there were other young women in the same sort of unbecoming pull-on, which flattened their heads and made their faces disproportionately large. Her green eyes grew huge, her cheeks flushed.

'Look,' she said.

Ed scanned the people sitting in the seats on his left. None of them remarkable, none of them known to him.

'What?' he said.

'There,' she whispered. 'Next row down, four, five, six seats away from you.'

He counted and looked.

An ordinary looking young man in a mac, like countless others. She'd probably met him at the shop, with Chapman, how was he expected to know?

'The man next to the girl with the cloak.'

'Friend of yours?' he said.

He looked again.

For some reason he felt uneasy, weak, lost. He couldn't think where the feeling came from, or what it was.

'He looks a bit like you,' she said.

His anger unaccountably subsided. He leaned across and kissed her cheek. She blushed. They were both behaving unlike themselves.

'Wonder if he limps too,' he teased her.

'God,' she said, ambiguously. She could have been countering his statement, or simply saying, 'Oh, dear.' She said, 'He's smiling at us.'

Ed turned. The ordinary young man was indeed looking over his right shoulder at them and grinning. Ed turned away and looked at the programme. But even so ordinary a movement seemed suddenly not to be part of him, disjointed. He had a sudden memory of those years ago in his childhood, wartime, was it, or even before, at any rate he was a small boy standing in front of a mirror, at first amazed that it copied everything he did, then annoyed, and then determined to catch it out. He had pretended not be be noticing anything, to be vague, distant, in a dream, and then suddenly and surreptitiously waggled the little finger of his left hand. The mirror caught him at it at once and did the same. He tried a fast, half-blink of his right eyelid. The mirror copied. Finally in desperation he banged on it, and when that had no effect (the mirror image simply imitated his passion) he picked up a chair (so did the boy in the mirror) and smashed the face. The relief was so great that he only remembered the release of it, and not what must have been his parents' anger and punishment. He had outgrown the mirror-despair, but this was something akin that he was unlikely to be able to shake off even when he was no longer in the presence of that ordinary man in a mac. With a sinking sensation he knew that even his thoughts might not be his own; had never been – but what did *that* matter until he knew about it? Was it Hamlet who had said, 'There is nothing either good or bad but thinking makes it so?' If so, then Hamlet knew what he, Ed, was now discovering. Knew that he was created. Is that what had driven him potty?

He heard distinctly inside his head every word he thought, spoken aloud twice, interlocking, so that so that he he might might never never be be able able to to think think straight straight again again.

He bent his head over the programme, a prickly warmth suffused his neck and ears, not because the man was looking at him – he had probably turned away by now and was studying the programme like himself – but because he now knew there would always be someone to read his most private inner feelings, thoughts, wishes.

'I'd just like to know what's going to happen, that's all,' Ed said aloud to his programme. 'I'd just like to know.'

'It's up to you,' she answered.

'I don't have much choice, do I?'

As usual they were each using arguments counter to their beliefs.

'You can choose,' she said uncertainly – 'I mean to a certain extent.'

108

'That's a contradiction in itself.'

He needed her at this moment as much as he'd ever done; needed her sanity, her ordinariness, her humanity. Needed her stupidity to tell him that his sharp-sensing intellect was faulty; needed her to bring him down to her level, and her earthiness.

'I could be killed on the way home, couldn't I?' he said; and waited for her common sense to stop his panic.

'You could.' She hesitated. 'But the chances are you won't. Come to that, you could kill yourself any time, but the chances are you won't.'

'What you're saying is,' Ed said, 'that the chances are equal – that there's no more chance of me getting run over on leaving here, than there is of me killing myself when I get home? You sound as if two follows one, and three follows two, and so on, and that it's extremely unlikely that 23 will suddenly follow seven. But life isn't like that. You know it isn't. 23 does follow seven any time, as often as three follows two. It's all chance.'

'Well I like it,' she said unexpectedly. 'Whatever it is.'

He was surprised.

'I don't,' he said.

'You don't think you like it, but you . . . you . . .' She would have liked to list the moments in every day that seemed to please him, or at any rate were certainly not unpleasurable – but she realised that happiness is an attitude, not the sum of the happy moments one has, but the recognition of them.

'You're too sensitive,' she said instead. 'You'd be happier if you weren't . . .'

'Sensitive my foot,' he said, 'the bad one.' And added: 'I'd love to know if the bastard limps.'

He decided to get up and leave, leave that face in the uniformity mac to register or improvise. Which came first, Eva's reaction and the mac's noting of it, or the mac's suggestive enquiry and Eva's response? Yes she would never have made a first move. She was a respondee – so, obviously, was the brainless offspring; but he at least (he clutched the programme tightly like a drowning man), had the ability to think and to do for himself. He eased forward as if to rise from his seat, and was caught in the dilemma of the thought that that man was actually manipulating him on a string.

Because he can't imagine what my reaction to the concert would be if I stay? Or because he recognises that my reactions may not fit into *his* scheme of things? Like a truant schoolboy, without looking either at his family or towards his tormentor, he edged along the row of seated people, and aimed for the exit. An icy wet fear ran through his veins, modulating to cool, but liquid as a deep reservoir, as he reached the exit and the stairs.

Eva saw Chris through a haze, through the water in her own eyes – and behind that blue she recognised herself to be a tenuous figment of another imagination . . . and was at the same time appalled and comforted by the thought. He looked so callow, so inexperienced – as part of his first attempt she knew she was bound to suffer . . . perhaps having learnt through her, he might get stronger, better, more acceptable. . . . She was willing to be part of his early mistake if she could believe he would have a second try; she willed him not to be too disappointed with the first – to use the experience he was gaining from it to make a second attempt . . . but he had Ed to contend with, and Ed was not the kind of man one could master; Ed was a self-made man who may as yet have achieved nothing, but who was on his way to enormities; enormities outside her comprehension. She felt she understood the young man in the mac better than she understood her own husband – and could love him more too, she admitted, partly because he was bound to fail in any trial of spiritual strength. He would not be adamant enough – whereas Ed would trample over whatever got in his way.

With painful awareness of what might be to come, she saw

through the watery film across her eyes, her child turn his head and raise two fingers of recognition at the same moment at which the young man in the mac turned his head towards him and smiled. 'Tony's recognised him,' she thought. 'How could he . . . unless he's waving at him because he looks like his father . . .'

She glanced across to the row below again, just caught Chris's smile as he turned away, and the blank regard of the girl next to him. 'She's looking straight through us,' she thought. She watched the girl turn away and link her arm through Chris's, smiling at him. She experienced a pang of jealousy. 'Wonder whether he'd give us up for her, or her for us, wonder which of us he values most?'

Ed's money was giving out; all sorts of extras he hadn't thought of diminished his savings by much more that the piano lessons and the concerts. Eva too was missing days at work, and in consequence pay, in her efforts to find them somewhere to live before the old building was demolished. She took long bus or Tube rides to track down advertised rooms, only to arrive too late or find the accommodation was not what was advertised, or was more expensive than advertised. She was now, with the earliest edition of the *Evening Standard* under her arm, queuing up for a phone booth near Shoe Lane, to speak to two advertisers whose phone numbers were printed by their 'Rooms to Let'. She had long since given up writing to Box No. so and so, because of the confusion arising in her mind from following up one enquiry whilst waiting for a reply to an earlier one.

When one call box was vacated, the first advertisement she decided to try was one which was oddly worded: 'One unpleasant room. Share b & k also unpleasant.' She dialled the number. It was either a misprint, she decided, or if it wasn't it was more than likely that what someone else considered unpleasant Ed would think just right. In any case, she'd tell something by what sort of voice answered the phone.

The voice was male, cultured, young.

'Have I got the right number,' she said. It didn't sound likely.

The voice was delighted to hear her, gave the address, said he'd be there till six o'clock this evening, and chatted, gaily, about the use of putting in such an advertisement.

'Couldn't bear to have someone in the room who didn't have a sense of humour . . . Three of you? Fine . . . we've got kids too . . .'

'The only thing is,' she said suddenly realising how far Camberwell Road was from Shepherd's Bush, 'it'd mean my husband changing his job . . . and I'd have to ask him . . .' She suddenly saw the whole project falling through.

There was a hiatus, and then the voice said, 'Come along anyway . . . if it doesn't suit don't worry . . . or he might find something this-a-way. Be seeing you.'

She gave over the phone box to the next comer and stood outside it for an hour, unable to make up her mind whether to go to see the room or not. How foolish of her never to have discussed with Ed the necessity, or not, of trying to find somewhere not too far from the café. And her own work too. How could she leave Chapman? And what on earth sort of work would she ever get somewhere else? She countered these thoughts with the fact that time was getting short, and she had tried first of all near home, and only gradually, as this seemed impossible, further and further away. Why haven't we *talked* about it? she wondered.

Well, Ed was absorbed with his work, his real work, and he probably had not thought about the giving up of their daily bread jobs; or perhaps he thought it was too obvious to discuss. Yes, they'd *have* to get somewhere near.

She saw all too clearly her inadequacy to deal with the most ordinary things of life. And yet he still treats me as if I *can* deal with them, and gets annoyed when I can't. He must think I'm brighter than I am. Eventually, half-heartedly, she took a Tube to the Elephant and Castle and enquired for Camberwell Road. It was a longer road than she had imagined, and, white with tiredness – 'I shouldn't feel like this, I'm only young – or not old anyway' – she took a short bus ride to get her nearer to the 200s.

When she did locate the right number she found it was a shop – selling linoleum, paint, do-it-yourself materials and wallpaper. She went inside. Yes, this is Number 281 . . . no, no rooms above here. She went outside and stood on the pavement – perhaps after all it was a practical joke. The voice on the phone could easily have been a hoaxer. . . . She stood undecided, then braving it went into the baker's next door. The older woman said yes it was next door, the wallpaper place. The younger woman disagreed. 'There's flats round the corner,' she said, 'they go from 250–300 – I know because I know someone who lives there.' Round the corner indeed was an iron staircase leading up to a concrete slab of gallery where were displayed dustbins and broken flower-pots. From the gallery, openings led into the dingy corridors. Eva waited in the dark of the first. She had no match to light. Eventually she heard something outside, and saw a small child. 'Number 281?' she asked. The child looked at her. She came out to look up and down the concrete path again. It was less dark and cold here than in the corridor. A woman called. The child turned and trotted back the way it had come. Eva followed. Her voice caught the woman unawares as she was about to slap the toddler on the back of its scraggy thighs.

'Can you tell me, Number 281?'

'It's at the end.'

The woman looked at her harshly, with dislike, as if she'd intruded on her own property. Eva went to the furthest opening, and called 'Hallo'. It echoed fearfully along the corridor.

There was no response. She thought she heard voices calling from the second door. She knocked. The voices seemed not to have heard, but to her surprise, the door was opened. A young woman looked at her without surprise, and said, presumably to the man behind her, though it seemed as if she were saying it to Eva, 'It's for you.'

The man in the corner of the room had a baby in his arms and a small child on either side of him.

'Ben!' she said as she turned away from the door.

Eva saw the tall young man with red hair get up from the bed.

'Hallo,' he said, 'I'll show you the room.'

As one of the small children had unaccountably started yelling, he picked it up (still with the baby under one arm) and, followed by the other child and the young woman, opened another door, and calling past his family said to Eva, 'It's up here.'

The way led from a small dark corridor and a flight of five or six steps. One room. It was, Eva saw at once, just what Ed would want. At the moment it was stuffed with packing cases, a bedstead, magazines, and broken dustbin lids, but it was big enough for a piano, a bed, a table, and the paraphernalia.

'We'll clear out all this,' said Ben.

He grinned at her.

She wanted to say, 'Oh no, please don't,' because Ed might find some of it useful, but embarrassment prevented her.

The man must have been in his mid-twenties. The girl, who was probably younger, looked ageless. Eighteen? Thirty?

'I like it,' said Eva.

'She'll want to see the kitchen and bathroom,' the girl said.

'Oh yes.'

They descended the few stairs again. In the small corridor, by the phone, Eva now noticed a gas stove.

'We cook here,' said Ben, 'and the bathroom's at the end. Actually the sink is in the loo, so it's not all that convenient.'

He took the few paces along the narrow passage and opened what looked like a cupboard door, revealing a lavatory and a basin.

'It's not really a bathroom,' said the girl, 'but it's where we wash.'

'Oh,' said Eva. 'How many share?'

'Only us,' she said.

'Yes.' Eva was not dismayed by the lack of a bath, though she was surprised. Where she now lived the bathroom did indeed have a bath but no one as far as she knew used it very often – too many people wanted to use the lavatory in it.

'You said about your husband's job,' Ben said pleasantly. 'What does he do?'

'Well, he serves in a café – he's a waiter,' she said limply, never having used the word waiter before. It sounded wrong somehow. Didn't suit.

'Could have a go around here . . . ?'

'I don't know,' she said, 'I'd have to ask him.'

Going back in the Tube she nearly cried with dismay at her own stupidity. How could she have said Ed was a waiter. Why hadn't she said 'musician'. The fact that he wasn't professional yet had nothing to do with it. He *was* a musician, who kept them going by working in a café. Perhaps she should phone Ben up and say he's not a waiter, he's a composer, but that would sound too ingratiating, and anyway why should they be interested?

'I'll tell him,' she decided, 'after I've spoken to Ed, and when I make another appointment, to tell them yes or no to the room.'

'You *can't* just move like that,' said Ed, 'unless you expect the café and Chapman to move with us – is that what you visualised?'

So, relieved, she went out to phone Ben to tell him, in case he got other enquiries this very evening and would put them off for her sake.

'We can't move because of work,' she said. 'Actually my husband is really a composer, but I work in a shop and I can't afford not to . . .'

'Cis has been making enquiries. There's a café along to the left, not far, that wants an evening worker. Male or female. 6 till 12. She mentioned you. So . . . just in case you change your mind . . .'

'Did you have other enquiries?'

'Enquiries, yes . . . but not serious ones. I mean a few people rang, but no one came.'

There was a pause. Strangely neither of them wanted to break the contact. Eva had already visualised herself taking Tony to that room, washing him in the basin . . . she kept the receiver to her ear.

'If your husband's a composer,' he eventually said, 'I'm sorry I didn't meet him.'

'Are you musical? I mean a musician?'

'No . . . I'm an actor. That is, when I can get work. I do other things in between.'

'Don't you want the café job?'

'No thanks,' he said politely, as if she'd found him a job. 'I'm in work at the mo.'

Eva reported the conversation to Ed. 'There's nowhere else,' she ventured, 'and I know you'd get on with them.'

'Why should I want to? The last thing I want is chat and socialising in the evening.'

It was true, he wanted somewhere where there was no chance of anyone being interested in what he was doing. He was like an inventor, jealously hugging to himself his project until he should be ready to launch it. In the rooms at Shepherd's Bush no one noticed the type of noise he made, no one bothered that Tony had a piano. They were 'the people below' just as, to them, the West Indian family was 'the people above'.

'You may want company,' he said. 'I expect you do. You've nothing else to do. But I want none of it.'

Her legs and whole body suddenly felt limp.

'I can't look any further,' she said. 'I'm worn out.'

'All right,' he agreed cheerfully. 'I'll do the looking.'

But half an hour later, thinking of his waning savings, and the waste of time and energy needed to look further, he went into the Bush, and phoned the Camberwell Road number.

'Too late if I come along now?'

'No,' said Ben. 'Any time.'

'I'm not paying out any more,' said Ed. 'I can't. The question is can you get us work? You heard the boy . . . and you've seen the sort of thing we do on stage. It's your move.'

'Well,' said Rudge unexpectedly. Ed wondered now why he'd been afraid to take the upper hand before. 'Well now . . . the first thing is to get you a card. The boy can get by without one poss-i-bly, but not you my friend. In fact,' he picked up the receiver, 'we'd better make sure of him too if we can . . . Get me Phillips,' he added into the receiver. He sat saying no more until the phone rang. Ed waited. He was at last going to find out what 'leave it to me' meant.

'Bob? Hallo there . . .' laugh . . . bonhomie, chat . . . rude joke, et cetera, 'listen Bob, I've got a man and a kid – anything on?'

For some reason Ed had a terrible picture of Burke and Hare raising his and Tony's bones from a graveyard. What were they going to be sold for, at twelve per cent he wondered. Rudge started his habitual biting of the quick around his index finger.

'M'm . . . m'm . . . could do . . . could be . . . Undistin-guished . . . 35-ish. The boy? Six . . . unappetising . . . you might have difficulty there – unless you need . . . uh-huh . . . uh-huh . . . uh-huh. . . . Right. I get you. Right . . . Thanks . . . 'Bye.'

'I don't hold out much hope,' he said to Ed, 'but there's

just a possibility. There's a loophole in Equity you see. Can't get into the profession if you want to be an actor even if you've trained three years and got a gold medal for it (of course they don't tell the kids this when they audition for the acting schools or the schools would be out of a job. Naturally). But you *can* get a preliminary card simply by doing one day's work on a commercial for TV. The Union doesn't bother whether you're a model, a would-be actor, or simply the man in the street with the right face . . . that's your way in.'

Ed waited.

'Bob *may* be able to get you something on a detergent or one of those lavatory cleaning commodities. He's an ideas man for a number of firms – and he doesn't let me down. However, your case isn't all that easy. . . .'

For the first two months after they moved to Camberwell Rudge didn't so much as answer the phone when Ed rang; and his silly secretary was capable enough to keep him from making an appointment.

'Sorry he's out of town this week; he's gone to Blackburn to see a client.'

'Sorry, Mr Rudge is away ill. Can I take a message?'

She didn't even ask his name after a bit, seemed to recognise it however much he disguised it.

'Sorry, Mr Rudge is out, can I get him to phone you back?'

And of course he didn't.

Before she was through the door she had said it. She stood with that awful knitted hat pulled down over to her brows, covering her ears. It was the hat he noticed most, when she said it; the hat that pinned the moment on to his retina; the moment he would remember.

'I'm pregnant,' she said. And smiled.

He stood stock-still, taking it in with the myriad thoughts and rearrangement of thoughts that accompanied the news. She caught his stillness, stood shocked at what she only now realised she had started, the train of talk that could not now be stopped.

It was not, of course, the news that had startled him. That could be dealt with. It was the fact that she had smiled, had taken the news in her stride as if it were something she would happily go through with. He felt her receding until she became a sharply focused distant point. The smile wiped off, but the badly knitted hat eternally in focus.

She stood as still as he, hoping by stillness to stave off the inevitable for one minute longer. Then stupidly, she said, 'Don't you want it now, Ed?'

He was aghast, opened his mouth and eyes like an actor showing to an audience how aghast he is. But he was not acting, she knew; he was being true to his own emotions which she recognised was the nearest approach to truth any of us reach. We arrange our thoughts to suit our tongues, but our feelings are more difficult to manipulate.

'Now?' he said. 'What's "now" got to do with it?'

She felt the rush of misunderstanding like a whirlpool envelope her; her misused 'now' dragging her down, swirling her around, while she flayed about uselessly.

Her 'now' had not meant 'You did once; have you changed your mind?' Which, of course, she saw now he had taken it to mean: an unjust accusation against himself. Yet what could she have done with that small word, where could she have put it, where it would not be the cause of such a misunderstanding. A long trail of words would have been necessary; painful, unsayable ones, to express what that little 'now' had meant to her, and in using it what she had expected it would have conveyed to him. Standing there in the doorway, the rush of knowledge of what she had meant could even yet have translated itself into words. 'Now. Now that Tony is normal. Now, now that you see we don't produce freaks. Now, now that you love him,' and as a whispered under-thought, 'now, now that I need someone to love as you love each other.'

But how could she bring herself to explain what she had meant, now that the 'now' had been said, and misinterpreted? Even now she believed that he did really know what she had meant, but was twisting her words either to hurt himself, or her, to show her how inept she was.

He said, quietly, viewing her at that distance, 'All right, don't abort, have it if that's what you want.'

'No, Ed. I thought . . . that . . .' Again the thing was inexpressible. '. . . I didn't think,' she ended feebly. 'I forgot.'

'Forgot!' Each ill-chosen word was dragging her further down, swirling her more swiftly towards the fall. She kept silent, but she wanted to scream: 'Yes, I forgot that my son was a moron! I forgot about not wanting another because my son is a moron!' But how could she have forgotten? She saw herself suddenly from Ed's point of view, at the wrong end of a telescope, pinpointed. How *could* I have forgotten? What have I been pretending to myself? Lulling myself with? That Tony is normal? Or that Ed thinks he is? She decided that the only thing to do was to leave her mind in its chaos, not attempt to smooth it out, but to return at once to the hospital and ask for an abortion. Having decided to do something, rather than think or speak, her mind switched to the next state of affairs as if there had been no drowning sensation a few seconds before. It shouldn't be a bad operation, I can't be far into pregnancy . . . (He saw her eyes flicker, and left her to her thoughts, turning away. It was her move next. If she didn't abort it was she who would suffer the consequences. He had repeatedly warned her.) . . . I don't really see how I can be pregnant at all, my periods are regular . . . but they say that *can* happen . . . if it does is it a sign that the child won't be normal? But that wouldn't matter now that I've decided not to have it . . . but anyway haven't I noticed (or semi-noticed without actually registering) that the last twice I've lost less blood than usual?

There were delays; she was told to come back, next week, the following week . . . then for an X-ray, then to pick up the X-ray . . . she began to have the pains again. 'Psychological,' she told herself, because of the fear . . . not of the operation, but because they might leave it too long and she'd have to have it and it would be a freak.

'Yaps,' said Rudge, 'a dog's dinner. 7 a.m. at Greek Street to get made-up and costumed, et cetera. Then they'll take you on to Hyde Park. Period piece.'

'What period?' asked Ed. He saw himself Edwardian, Victorian, Regency, but felt a cold embarrassment at the thought that he might be asked to dress up in tights with bloomers, or, worse still, in a cod-piece.

'Period,' repeated Rudge, as if there were only one, and Ed were a fool not to know anything so elementary, and adding wittily the American full-stop 'period'.

'You'll get £15 and the boy £15. Unless the director picks either of you out to do something special (close-up, solo moment, speaking or such-like) in which case you'll inform me at once, and you'll get a lot more. My fees are fifteen per cent of the total.' He hurried his words in case Ed should interrupt, conscious of the fact that he had told Ed he'd take twelve per cent of the boy's money 'because he's a child' but had not mentioned the percentage for Ed's work.

'We'll have to put you together as an act because, of course, you don't exist separately, and you couldn't in any case get any form of entertainment job other than what the boy will provide you with – and as a matter of fact I'm doing you a great favour in using you as well as Tony for a commercial, to enable you to get at least a preliminary union card. So,' he concluded, '7 a.m. Tuesday 23rd, at Greek Street, and keep in touch.'

Eva stood white in the doorway. Why did she never wait until she was inside the room with the door discreetly closed behind her, before blurting out whatever it was she wanted to say? She stood there, forcing him to look at her. She removed the knitted cap, no doubt realising for the first time that it offended him.

'They want to see you,' she said.

'Who?' It entered his mind that Ben was going to turn them out – that his temperamental wife was objecting to Tony's practising, or his Destructo sounds, although he had assured Ed only last week that it never woke their children, and they themselves weren't bothered by noise.

'Who?' he repeated.

'The hospital.'

He was surprised.

'Me? When?'

'Tuesday, between eight and eleven.'

She came into the room as if that were that; that she'd done her part and it was now up to him. Was she really unaware? Or had she once more 'forgotten', as she seemed so conveniently to do whenever there was anything of importance in their lives?

Quietly, he said, as she listlessly threw the knitted cap on to the bed and sat by it, 'You *would* choose the only day....'

Sensing that some upheaval was once more on the way, she forestalled it by crying out in anguish, '*I* didn't choose it.'

He was amazed at her vehemence; at her whole fraught aggressive attitude. He replied gently, 'No, of course you didn't, but how *can* I?'

It was a moment before she realised that Tuesday was *the*

Tuesday. *The* Tuesday. The one day in the year when, of course, he couldn't. The one day they had been talking about, planning for, since early that month. She buried her face in the pillow, hot with shame that she could once more have forgotten the most important things in his life, in Tony's. She had been so preoccupied with her earlier mistake, so eager to put it right for him; but she had only succeeded in making things worse. She had been absorbed with her own pain, and fright that she might after all have to have the child which she knew now could only be a freak. She had been living with her fear and her pain, and forgotten them, forgotten those who were her life, the only beings who meant anything to her, the only people she was alive for.

He sat by her, and smoothed her hair.

After a while she said, 'I can phone and alter the appointment.'

'If you really think it's necessary for me to go at all?' he asked.

'Well ... they said ...'

He got up.

Slowly she sat up too. Combed her hair; pulled the cap on over her ears, looked in her purse for the necessary change, and went out.

'We're living apart,' she thought. 'Our bodies live in one room, but our lives are far apart.'

She wondered whether she really cared any more. 'I'm too tired,' she decided, 'to care whether I care or not ...'

Now ... how the hell am I going to manipulate the hospital – this hospital in W.12 with another one near Camberwell Road? What forms will I have to fill in, what contrivances will I have to use to get her into hospital there, to get Ed there ... Why in any case did I want to move her from Shepherd's Bush to Camberwell? Was there a reason? And if I don't move her – if I cut out all that bit about the advertisement, and Eva's meeting with Ben, will I have to put it back later, because later in the book I may see the real reason why I put it in? And if this is so, how will I cope with what I will have put between? Will I have to cut all that, or re-do it into another meaning, not so evident but more expedient? Shall I . . . Shan't I . . . shall I . . . shan't I . . . ?

If I shut the door on Camberwell, what of the future I shall also be shutting the door on? The real, underlying necessity to their lives of this move? Aberration or fundamental necessity? They were perhaps one and the same thing. I shall therefore have to bring them (have brought them) to Camberwell. Decision made.

The fact that I've arbitrarily made Ben an actor may be the clue to why they moved. But why move to meet him? Any pub in Shepherd's Bush would have done.

'You don't have to get up.'
'I'll get the breakfast.'
'I'll get it. Stay in bed.'
She stayed, reluctantly. It was a much greater effort to stay than to get up. But getting them their breakfast this morning would look like interference, as if Ed were not capable. She was conscious of it being their day, she didn't want to intrude into it – simply to make sure that Tony was properly buttoned, and was taken to the lavatory.

'Come on lazybones. Work.' This was to Tony, who bleary-eyed with unfulfilled sleep wanted to be left in the warmth of unconsciousness. It was twenty to six. They would be gone in half an hour and she'd have a whole day to get through alone with her fears and the pain in her stomach. What time would they be back? she wondered. Indiscreet to ask. Probably late afternoon. Should she perhaps go surreptitiously to Hyde Park and watch from a distance, where he couldn't see her? Would she be able to lie afterwards to him, or would he be angry if she told him she'd been there, watching? She formulated a half-lie. 'I thought I'd come and watch but I didn't find you.' It might prove true anyway. Comforted that she might see them later she lay back again.

The make-up man addressed the hairdresser without looking at him.

'Well, what am I supposed to do with this one then?'

'Don't ask me.'

He glanced over at Tony in the dentist-like chair.

'They'll have to find a hat as far as I'm concerned,' he said.

'We've got a cap for him,' said the young girl who was doling out clothes from a pile into Ed's arms, and talking to herself as she handed them over. 'Check waistcoat, brown coat, grey trousers, there's the cap for the boy, boy's trousers, jackets, what size shoes does he take?'

'I don't know,' said Ed.

'Try these. Shall I dress him?'

'Yes. Okay.'

A small fat-faced girl with ringlets, already dressed in pantaloons and a check gingham dress, came from behind the rail of clothes.

'Is this all right?'

'No, dear, the bow is wrong. I'll take it off for you. And you can't wear those shoes. I'll give you some boots, what size are you?'

'Three and a half,' said the girl promptly. 'If you mean grown-up size.'

'Try these.'

Tony, Ed thought, looked ludicrous with the red-brown

stuff sponged over his face, and the powder which had inadvertently whitened his eyelashes.

He cringed mentally and physically with the knowledge that the same stuff was about to be applied to his own face. Should he behave jollily, nonchalantly, as if he were used to it – or should he simply sit and keep quiet, taking whatever was done to him as the price for which he was being paid. He felt nauseated, as if he were being sent to a slaughter-house, rather than to a day's work as an actor for good pay.

He went through a panic of self-consciousness as the cast was shepherded down the stairs into Greek Street and into a small van 'The sound van,' said the ringleted little girl – where, among a lot of equipment, tubes, wires, booms and boxes, they sat upon a wooden bench placed down one side of the van.

There were seven of them, an elderly man (he had simply been an old man in Ed's mind when he'd first seen him this morning, but dressed in his period clothes, with white sideboards pasted on to his face, he now looked distinguished enough to be thought of as elderly), a spinster-ish looking woman whose thinness was exaggerated by the clothes, who was pulling on some white mittens; a more homely-looking woman, a sharp-looking young man, and the ringleted child.

It was half past eight when they got out of the van near Marble Arch and trundled, the boom operator leading the way, the women picking up their skirts, across a wide expanse of short damp grass, under a drizzle of rain. They came to a halt near a pathway, where under a tree the director and camera-lighting man were sheltering. Under a nearby tree the camera was protected by a mackintosh cover, and huddling by it were two younger men, both in knitted caps not unlike Eva's, but more colourful and with unattractive pom-poms, too large, perched on them. Only the director took any notice of the tramping arrivals.

'Let's sort it out while we wait for a bit of daylight, shall we?' he said, facing the desultory crowd from his partly-sheltering tree, but leaving them in the open. Ed was glad of his bowler, of his elastic-sided boots, and of his waistcoat. The morning was chill, and he realised that if they had all been called upon to perform in nothing but bathing briefs, they would have been no more cosseted than they were now being.

'Yes,' the director was saying, 'let's try these three as a family. See if it makes sense.'

He beckoned to the ampler of the two women to stand by Ed, and called out, 'Come on, darling, yes, you there with the ringlets, come and be their little girl.'

He squinted at the three of them.

'Look as if you know each other at least,' he said.

The small girl smiled up at Ed, with a taught, advertisement expertise. He scowled back at her.

'Put your arm around her – no, you fool, not her waist, her shoulder, across her shoulder. M'm. Possible.'

From a short distance a dog barked. A beautiful, well-washed Collie, fit for Cruft's, held on a rope by a handler.

'There's our star,' said the director proudly. 'Hallo, there, my star, good morning to you,' he called.

The handler and dog started moving towards him.

'No, don't get him wet, you bloody idiot,' he called.

The handler retreated, and the dog continued to bark.

The director nodded at the 'actors'.

'You can find yourselves a tree or two,' he said, 'we won't be starting yet.'

It sounded simple enough. Through a megaphone the first assistant bellowed at the sheltering trees his own interpretation of what the director was saying. As the director changed his mind, the bellower re-shouted the orders, as if the waiting cast had stupidly misunderstood his previous pronouncements.

'*Not* in a circle; *not* in a circle. You'll sit in a *semi*-circle. Don't unpack the hamper, you there in pink, repeat *don't* unpack the hamper, it will be already unpacked.'

'You, darling . . .' to the ringlets '*not* from behind that tree, from further away – no *not now*, later . . . I'll show you where from later . . .'

When the stretch of park had been emptied of onlookers by the downpour, and only the whoosh of distantly discernible traffic could be heard, the camera-lighting man emerged from his tree, his brolly and his duffle-hat, squinted upwards through his spy glass, and said morosely, 'Oke.' The shouting and rush began – Ed and his 'wife' were told to sit on the pooled grass – the ringleted girl was taken by the hand to a distant tree and told to skip 'when I *tell* you, not before' at top speed towards her family. The picnic was laid out, the hamper lid left open.

'Can't use the boy,' said the director. 'Get him out of the way. Come on, let's rehearse. Go on, *eat – smile* – look as if it's a great day. Come on, ringlets. For Christ sake tell ringlets to come.'

About ten yards from her picnicking 'parents' the small girl slipped on the sodden grass, splayed her legs outwards, cried out in shame and pain, and her face downwards, burst into tears.

'For Christ's sake,' said the director again.

'I've broken my foot, I've broken my foot!' cried the child.

'I think she's twisted her ankle, Bob.'

'O.k. take her to a hospital. We'll have to use the boy. Sorry, kid. All right, save the eating, we'll have to try something else.'

'Sun's gone again,' said the camera-man.

'Right. You boy. Go to the hamper. Take out the dog's dinner. No, put it back. Take out the dog's plate. Now the dinner. No, Roger – have the dinner already in the plate will you? Right . . . now take out the plate, come on bring it here, right here, nearer. Right? There. Now, when I say action that's what you'll do. Right? Have we got the dog ready? Good. Count two, no three, after action and then let her go. Is she hungry enough? Right, we'll rehearse it. Action. Boy! Action! Right. Bring it here. No! Put it on the ground. Right . . . let him go, Steve, let the dog *go* for Christ's sake, it should be almost simultaneous.'

The dog amicably ambled towards the food, sniffed delicately at it, declined it, and turned to put his paws on Tony's shoulders as an expression of gratitude, and contrition at not being hungry enough to accept the kindness. Tony yelped – ran – fell – screamed – the dog followed tail-wagging – stood over him – smiling – tongue out like a pink flag of friendliness.

Ed remained seated. He felt no sense of betrayal. If the director yelled at the boy, if the boy shook with fear, he felt no need, no faint compulsion to interfere. He wanted his temporary card, and his payment; he was not going to walk out on either of these necessities. If he was dismissed he guessed that Rudge would have a case; if he went voluntarily he would forfeit the possibility.

He was dismissed.

By the time he had collected his damp and pulp-faced son, found his own way back across the grass to a taxi (a public conveyance would have been more than he could face), had got the boy home and undressed, and the anachronistic clothes tied into a bundle and delivered back, this time by public transport, to Greek Street – by the time he had phoned Rudge and got no reply, it by this time being well after seven o'clock at night, he had only one thought in his head. He would get a card – albeit a temporary one. And so would Tony. No doubt the dog had one too, but possibly for a different, more respected, though possibly just as overcrowded, union.

If this were compromise, be it so. If this were expediency he had no fear of it. Let anything serve. What shocked him was not his personal compromise, but the ignominy, the cruel and tacit assumption that he was not good enough to advertise dog food. But he clung to the other face of compromise, telling himself that in his case it was not expediency, it was the paving for his future hopes, his possibility of presenting his view and feel of life to any other human response. No, not even that; the human response was not really the basic necessity, it was the right and ability to create that mattered. These middlemen, agents, Yap-sellers, lowest slaves of all that he most abhorred were his stepping-stones to the new possibility.

There had been a time when Ed had wished it on her, silently willed it, although afraid at the same time that it might happen; afraid that it might happen because he had wished it, but been unable to backtread the thought – and been glad that he had been unable to.

Had he too, then, a mere creature, the power over someone else's life? And death? How much power? More, or less, than he had over his own? Or over the tiniest detail of his own.

What happens, he had decided then, was not of his doing – he had believed neither in prayer nor telepathy, nor in any power that thought might have. Thus he exonerated himself, absolved himself from murder by wish.

Lately, the one-time comfort of her presence had become an irritant; he no longer needed her even in order to destroy her; she had passed on to her son her sense of the formality of tradition, of the tradition of form – the boy would now do for Ed's purposes.

And now, now, it was all happening as he knew it would, as he had always half-sensed, as he had progressively wanted. And though the sophisticated side of him had pushed aside the shape of the future, telling him that he was powerless to alter it, his primitive senses had known that this would be so, that this was to be the shape of it, that without this, shapelessness would not be achieved. He had always subconsciously, secretly, known, but never before joyously and

130

openly admitted to himself, that it had all started the day he was born, which was at the beginning of time, and would go on happening as long as he was here, which he always would be. He'd always known that time ran continuous and contiguous with himself, that he could lift the veil on bits of it here and there at random and at will, when it suited his purpose.

He recognised that the continuum was too vast for his comprehension, but that it was not there except through his comprehension. He saw himself as the only and total creator . . . that is why, after a brief vertigo of panic at the concert hall, he had realised that it was his own sense of the ironic that was seeing that man in the mac as outside his will. The man in the mac was the Red King who might wake up and blow him to bits, but he himself was not only Alice, who was imagining the Red King, but Lewis Carroll as well, and not only Lewis Carroll but the mind who had created him.

As he and the boy walked along the passage between the rows of beds in the long, women's ward, he knew that he was setting in motion his own wish to get rid of Eva and all she stood for, now.

What happened after destruction didn't matter. It was the releasing of his physical mental spiritual and sexual urge to destroy that dominated any vague thought of his or her afterlife. He had already experienced the stunted outcome of his sexual urge, but could no more have resisted that drive even had he known that the result was to be Tony, than he could contain his destructive need because its result might be an annihilation of other living things.

He heard her say, propped white and tensed against the pillows – 'I don't mind . . . it doesn't matter,' as if mind and matter had the same signficance, as if she had reconciled them both to his will. But there remained something outside his will, which irritated like sand in an oyster shell . . . a fundamental relationship between the woman and the child which he could neither enter nor destroy, which neither her death nor his talent had power over. Mock it as he would he could not get rid of it. It was present now in a communion of non-words, in neither touch nor look, but in a felt knowingness that ran between them as surely as any demonstrable sign of life. Because it was indefinable it was untouchable; he could think it, exorcise it, feel it, be driven mad by it, but its sense lay outside what he could humanly do to it.

Somewhere, somehow, through all the unbearable excesses of Bosch's imagination, and concentration camp fact, this feebly thin all-powerful thread remained and would remain unassailable. Nor by willing her cancerous death, could he eradicate it. She would leave its mark behind her on the moronic boy.

The willed death of his wife had to do with his most hidden pysche, but it had also to do with the outward manifestation of his art, or, since the word 'art' had such appallingly out-moded connotations, with Destructo as he preferred to call it.

He was irritated rather than solaced by the realisation that it was probably not only his will that had killed her. She must, he supposed, have carried within herself the germ of her own destruction before he met her. He was surprised and pleased at his own adaptability (perhaps the weeks she spent in hospital had prepared him), certainly he had no feeling of loss or even of change after she was gone. It was as if she had not been, or had been a part of his half-remembered child-hood, or a character in a book he had read the year before last.

He continued to concentrate on his son . . . undecided as yet, how, or even whether, he wanted to destroy him, or tor-ture him, or simply challenge him. Tony, unlike Eva, would fight for life, would cling to his apprehension of form and music, would shut out the noise and the fall until the last possible moment. Although Ed was in no doubt that he would eventually win, he knew the boy's defences to be formidable – indeed he needed them to be to achieve his coup. There would be no orgasmic relief in destroying a weakling – that was why he had known that Rudge was instinctively right when he insisted that Tony have lessons . . . the child must be poised between the strengths of real ability and untouched purity, before he was ready for the fight. Ed even felt he might grow to love his adversary. . . .

But he had to have patience. Between the bouts of piano-playing which, far from suffering from Eva's death, seemed to have gained from it in delicacy of performance – the boy was impossible to live with. He was a closed and swollen-faced numbskull. His hatred of his father showed itself more overtly than any human mood he had been able to convey since his birth. As if he knew, could see into Ed's very skull, could point a finger at the shapeless thought that had wished his mother to death.

The act would become a duel. Whether the boy was conscious of it or not, instead of immersing himself in his playing and trying to ignore the Destructo interruptions that Ed practised upon him nightly, his playing sang out challenge. He heard the falling clatter, was aware now that it was done to destroy him, and instead of collapsing as he used to in savage misery when it broke his cherished harmony, he firmly and antagonistically brought his playing to a *fortissimo* that it was difficult to believe could come from his small fingers. He had, to Ed's relief, not yet been shown the pedals, nor in fact, without getting off his stool would he have been able to reach them. Ed recognised him now not as a skittle that he himself had purposely set up but as a determined and forceful opponent.

Drowning his sound, or at least the sense of it, was not a great difficulty, but overcoming him audibly was not Ed's aim. His aim was to reach his nerve-centre; and he realised now that it would take more ingenuity than he had hitherto had to employ. He didn't resent the battle – in fact he welcomed it. Looking back the fight had been too one-sided; the victory too easy. Instead of an entertainment the act would now have a more desperate base, spectators would be forced, not morally but emotionally, to take sides, those taking the weaker being eventually overwhelmed with the weaker performer. And, as Ed knew, there was never going to be a chance that the weaker one would be himself.

Rudge was increasingly unapproachable now that he had signed the contract, and got him a preliminary card. He was deeply offended by Ed's behaviour at his TV commercial; Ed had 'let him down', he had 'put himself out' and 'been made a fool of' and, having got this message across to Ed (he didn't want to hear that it was Tony not Ed who had behaved badly), he wasn't going to do any more for them.

Ed discussed it with Ben.

'They're all the same,' said Ben consolingly. 'They get you on their books, but they've nothing to offer. How could they have with ninety-two per cent of actors out of work. The most they, and you, can hope is that you'll land yourself a job and give them ten per cent of the proceeds.'

'Fifteen,' said Ed.

Ben shrugged, 'How long did you sign up for?'

'Three years.'

Ben shrugged again.

'But it's the only three years I've got,' said Ed. 'The boy will be useless after that.'

'I'll keep my ears open for you.'

'Ben . . .' Cis came into the room complainingly, he was always evading her, talking to someone else, showing off his cheerful façade when he knew and she knew that there was nothing beneath it but the possibility of failure . . . 'I've been calling for you.'

'See you,' said Ben, waving an actorish hand at Ed. . . . Cis shut the door of Ed's room before she handed him the card.

Typed were the words: '10 a.m. Tuesday, Crown & Anchor, Dean Street; 2.15 p.m. Wednesday: Dinely Studios, Marylebone Road.'

'It's Tuesday tomorrow,' she said, 'and it's already 4.30.'

'She may still be in the office!'

He dialled four times to no reply; though after the first time he knew it was no use. He'd have liked some clue as to what the auditions were for, and she wouldn't be in the office by 10 a.m. tomorrow. Nevertheless, he felt light-hearted, young, unburdened by Cis's pessimism, or children, or having to earn money. He sang to himself as he went back to the room. 'Hey diddle de dee, an actor's life for me.'

'I couldn't do that,' Ed thought, listening for the twenty-third time that evening to the same words, as Ben's voice carried through the thin wall to the upper room.

'The foul fiend haunts poor Tom in the voice of a nightingale. Hopdance cries in Tom's belly . . .' 'Lurk, lurk.'

> 'As I stood here below, methought his eyes
> Were two full moons; he had a thousand noses,
> Horns whelk'd and waved like the enridged sea:
> It was some fiend . . .'

'No, I couldn't do that,' he repeated emphatically. 'Couldn't repeat the same words night after night.'

To repeat them till he knew them, yes, that might be possible, though his own method of work was opposed to this. His own work depended on its unrepeatability. Ben's work was to take an author's score and repeat it over and over to whoever paid to hear. But what of Ben himself, the interpreter. Was not the repetition so numbing that the repeater lost all sense of meaning, and eventually only presented the form of form without content?

He took the opportunity when he heard Cis's voice, blurred with sleepiness, cry out, 'Shut up! For God's sake that's enough. Shut up, shut up, shut up!' Tony was asleep . . . he opened the door, padded down the few stairs and knocked. Ben said, 'Sorry. . . . I'm shutting up now.'

'No,' said Ed, 'I don't want to sleep, it isn't . . .'

Ben's eyes shone: 'Will you hear me?'

'I did.'

'I mean will you hear my lines – hold the book and prompt.'

'That's what I was going to . . .'

They went up the stairs. Tony was undisturbable. They sat on the bed.

Was this why? Was this to lead to the why? Why people moved, or why people moved people? The paperback now in Ed's hands smelt of future necessity . . . he would see, in time, why he, Chris, had moved Ed, so seemingly unnecessarily, to Camberwell. He could smell the printed paper, feel it through Ed's hands – it pointed the way to a future page which would reveal the why. In the meantime all he had to do was to go on copying out Edgar's lines from his own paperback. The lines themselves were significant of so many things. Whoever wielded them would be able to turn them to account. He was on Ed's side about repetition. His own work demanded the same once-and-for-allness, but he hadn't yet allowed Ben to speak, to explain what it was that made it possible – even desirable . . . how can I know whose side I'm on till I see what they say, he thought, even if it is I who will put their thoughts into their mouths, and on to paper?

'Let but the herald cry,
And I'll appear again . . .'

Even out of context it heralded something, somewhere, that one had heard or sensed before . . . or would do in the future.

136

> 'The gods are just, and of our pleasant vices
> Make instruments to plague us . . .'

'Frateretto calls me; and tells me Nero is an angler in the lake of darkness. Pray, innocent, and beware the foul fiend.'

Involuntarily Ed glanced over his shoulder towards his sleeping son. Neither he nor Eva had ever taught him to pray. Ed would have scoffed at such stupidity, but was sure nevertheless that Eva had not tried, even behind his back. She had no doubt prayed for the boy herself, but had not filled his small-capacitied brain with such an outlandish idea.

'Pray, innocent, and beware the foul fiend.' The words tickled him. Tragedy did tickle, there was no denying it.

No, this sense of the future wasn't the reason, or rather it was not the only reason, why Ed had moved. There was at least one more, and this one more tangible, more positive. It was because of Karl; so that he, Ed, would be around when Ben heard, in one of the rehearsal rooms, of Karl.

'The only thing is – he's deaf.'

'For Christ's sake, one doesn't make music for the deaf!' shouted Ed – but later asked himself if this was quite true. An introduction to an impresario, however phoney, however deaf, was a step in some direction.

Karl, in fact, had a hearing-aid which he put in superciliously when he first met people. He always took it out when auditioning, or watching an act. He was a master impresario, as original and dynamic as anyone in the field; and so narrow and eclectic in his tastes that he had waited six years to get together a show that pleased him enough to present it. Not that the acts he chose could afford monetarily to hang around without work for all that time.

When he found something that appealed to him (and it need only be a bare idea, he himself would elaborate it into an act) he paid an outright sum in return for which he made his future actors sign a slip of paper guaranteeing that that particular act was his property. None of them made any objection – partly because the idea was in most cases only developed into a sellable act by Karl himself, and partly because he commanded a certain amount of fear. Nor did they feel bound. They were perfectly free to perform other acts anywhere they could until such time as he would have a show big enough to launch. He met Ed by appointment in a bus shelter along Watford Way.

It was a drizzly day, cold and uninviting, and as the rain slanted down upon them, the roof under which they sat provided no shelter at all. Karl nodded as Ed approached, evidently in no doubt that this was the man who had contacted him, and ostentatiously adjusted his hearing-aid.

Ed began: 'It's difficult to explain . . .'

'Good for a start,' said the man admiringly, 'go on from there.'

Ed elaborated.

The man listened. 'Possible, possible,' he said to himself. He told Ed that he already had four acts signed on, he needed a fifth . . . 'For a one-hour show. So, with any luck, I should be able to start soon. I'll have to locate the others if yours fits (or if yours doesn't, when someone else's does), they're all dispersed . . .' he seemed to be talking to himself, he had taken out his hearing-aid.

'You should have brought the boy.'

'Yes.'

'Bring him tomorrow and show me.' He gave the address.

'Well,' said Ed, 'there's rather a lot to transport.'

The man shrugged and dismissed the subject.

It was obviously up to Ed to come or not as he chose – perhaps he hadn't even heard, or read his lips. He had already given a nod of recognition to his next appointment, a young woman with hair dyed the yellow of a soft boiled egg.

So, there was nothing for it, he'd have to get a taxi from Camberwell to Greenwich, he'd never locate a van free to take him and his stuff at such short notice.

'I must be mad,' Ed thought. The taxi was flicking up to £2 when the driver assured him 'just round the corner from here'.

Strapped on the roof grid, and by the driver, and impeding his and the boy's view completely, were his props. Not all of them – the heaviest he had had to leave behind – but he reckoned on finding some form of replacements in the pub – including, of course, a piano.

Ed's anxiety about the money he was laying out decided him to find Karl before unloading, and insist that he pay – although of course he realised he had no right to. He found Karl with difficulty, sitting alone in a large empty upstairs hall, still in his mackintosh. He got up and came downstairs at once with Ed, though he had not got his earpiece in, so had no chance of hearing Ed's complaints. Ed transferred his purse from his jacket to his trouser pocket, preparatory to showing Karl the empty linings when the taxi driver should want to be paid. They spent a long time getting the stuff upstairs; the driver was willing, though not with pleasure or alacrity, to unload, but not to leave the pavement. As the last article was taken out of the cab, without demur Karl opened a continental-type purse and deposited some paper money into the driver's hand. They both seemed to accept the transaction without so much as verifying what had passed between them. Ed relaxed, a smile twisted one side of his lips. He was eager now to show off his act.

Karl stood on the pavement and said, 'Where's the boy?'

Ed looked about him quickly, head movements like a nervous long-legged bird – he couldn't surely have got back into the taxi without them noticing when it left.

Karl led the way upstairs, opened the door of the lavatory at the top of the stairs and said 'No.' He led the way into the long empty room. The piano was at one end, by the window, but no boy. Ed cursed. He began placing his props where he wanted them; it was a slow operation. Karl went downstairs.

'Seen a boy?'

'A boy?' said an old woman with a bucket.

'Have you seen one?'

'Just given him some chips,' she said.

'Where?'

'Round behind the bar there.'

Karl retrieved him, said to the woman on his way back upstairs, 'Where can I wash his hands?'

'Here you are,' she said. She proffered the bucket. 'I haven't started yet.'

She dipped the salt-sticky fingers into her bucket and wiped them on her apron. Tony took a huge intake of breath. The reminder of what a woman was, how a mother behaved, filled his lungs with a desire to bawl like a baby. He held his breath, decided to concentrate only on men and boys to avoid the pain, and stomped up the stairs behind Karl without looking back.

'Let's hear him,' Karl said, 'first.'

Tony sat at the piano, an old upright, which still sounded surprisingly good, and started to play.

'No,' Ed cut him short almost at once, 'begin with the short piece, then this . . . like we did this morning.' Tony complied.

Ed spoke through it to Karl. 'At this moment, I will seem like a stage-hand, placing the props. Like an interruption that's perhaps meant, perhaps not, but certainly an irritation to the audience. He'll be dressed up by the way, dinner-jacket, or velvet suit or what-have-you . . .'

'You should come on,' said Karl, 'round about now – not earlier, and contrive to look as if you've mislaid something – mutter "excuse me" to the world in general, and hang around a bit – then see the first prop you want. O.k. Let's go back and rehearse the timing of the opening.'

They worked for two hours, to Ed's great satisfaction. The young man had an undeniable flair, musically, in spite of his deafness, and visually, beyond Ed's imaginative abilities.

He was particularly clever with the child, who had retired inside his emotionalism and was playing like an automaton so as not to have his equilibrium disturbed. When it came to impregnability Tony was a fortress; but where Ed would have attacked head on ferociously, Karl went softly, insidiously, towards breaking him; and each time breaking point was near, switched kindly and firmly to another piece of music, so as not to forestall results that were best left unrehearsed.

He had suggested an ambulance siren and an antique plaster cast Venus as additional props ('I'll get them for you') but it was only when they were packing up to go that he suddenly called to Ed –

'I've got it! A pistol shot! One, one only.'

How could this unattractive young man with the thin white mackintosh and cumbersome hearing-piece who met his prospective 'artistes' in a bus shelter, aspire to paying them any money at all, let alone the minimum accepted by their union? And if indeed he was attempting to employ them outside the union, why had he made sure at that first meeting that Ed had at least a preliminary card. Ed was by now so eager to perform that he stifled his impatience to talk about money, as they went up and down the stairs after the audition, which Karl called the 'séance', as it was certainly not for him auditory.

It was, in fact, he who mentioned payment.

'Shall I send the retainer on to your agents?'

Ed said 'No' at once, this was nothing to do with Rudge, but changed his mind and gave the agent's address. After all, he might want legal help if a contract was to be made, and he supposed if he were to break into a profession, he might as well start by behaving professionally, however much it irked him.

Also, of course, it might impress Rudge to have a fee sent him on behalf of a client he had no hopes of. It was this last consideration that decided Ed, although at the same time he loathed this vestige in his nature of the wish to impress which had attacked him and been regularly repulsed as a child.

In fact, only seven weeks passed before Karl had got his whole show together. He had found all the acts out of work except one, whose engagement on a tour of working men's clubs (though not, of course, with the specific act he had bought) held up the opening. Ed had supposed that the show was to run at least a week, he had not heard of one-night stands, but apart from the payment he had to admit that a once-and-only would suit his act.

He arrived at the pub as ordered at a little before 9 on the day of the night and was told to store his equipment in the passage outside the room where dark brown kitchen chairs with rounded backs were being put along three walls – three deep. There wasn't going to be much room for the performers.

Throughout the day the various acts arrived with their costumes and props; cramped space on stage and off was found for all of them by Karl – Ed brought his stuff piece by piece to the window as he was told, blocking out the light, but leaving enough space for the piano-stool. He lunched with the boy and some of the actors downstairs in the pub, but although there was time to spare he didn't want to go out. Air and light had nothing to do with what they were preparing here. Upstairs Karl closed and bolted the shutters.

As the time drew near, make-up and costumes were put on, and he dressed the boy, who still refused to dress himself, in the appalling Little Lord Fauntleroy suit Karl had provided for him.

Half an hour before the scheduled opening time, Ed left the

communal make-up-and-dressing room and came out on to the landing. He saw Karl approaching the top of the stairs with difficulty carrying, dragging, pushing and manipulating a small wheel-chair. Ed grinned.

'For me?'

'No. That is . . .' – he gave the first smile Ed had seen on his face – 'I doubt it.'

He had got the chair over the top step and on to the landing by now, and was wheeling it towards the hall. Ed stood, contemplating what he might do with it, given the chance. He was wondering whether its height would be suitable for the piano – or whether sitting in it, the boy would be unable to reach the keyboard . . . Karl had gone down the stairs and was coming up again, this time carrying a thin old woman who, in spite of her plastered make-up, henna'd hair and blood-red talons, had the aspect of a nervously captured but still voracious bird of prey. Ed followed Karl into the hall and watched as he placed his burden into the wheel-chair and covered the bones that were legs with a white crotcheted baby's shawl. Ed saw him bend over the old head as if lip-reading. The lips of the painted crone moved, but no words came. They understood each other. After a minute Ed left the doorway, not that they were aware of him, and waited in the passage by the lavatory. He caught Karl as he was about to go down the stairs.

'What an act!' he said admiringly, over-moving his lips, but speaking quietly as Karl had no earpiece and he didn't want to be overheard. 'What does she do?'

'Do? Nothing . . .'

'You mean that's all she does? Just sit there?' Ed was disappointed.

Karl rubbed his fingers and thumb together.

'She forks out,' he said quietly, and added as he turned away, 'unnecessarily hugely as it happens.'

The audience began to arrive quietly, not sure that they should be there – glad that they weren't the only ones.

Karl handed out sheets of paper ('20p, please') and one after the other the audience bought them; either as they came in, or coming back after they were seated. They saw each other's, grinned, shrugged and bought just the same. Those who hung back finally joined in out of embarrassment. And yet, apart from the first two or three buyers, they all knew, could see, that there was nothing on the paper. The sheets were blank; but the actions and repeated words of Karl, his very presence, drew them into performing their part of the pointless ritual. Some of them not only joined in the joke, but carried it further, reading aloud the blank paper to each other, pointing out words, turning the paper over to read the other side, putting on spectacles; humouring each other, appeasing Karl, wanting to be part of it, with it, in the know-how.

The first act was screened off before the audience arrived; Ed had paid little attention to his fellow artists so had no idea who was there until two girls took the screens away.

A huge ventriloquist doll sat a man on his knee. The doll had that appalling red pillarbox slit of a mouth, hard brilliant eyes and jerky head movements of his kind. The man on his knee was a mild fellow in a dinner-jacket (the doll was, of course, dressed in an Eton jacket and stiff collar) who smiled deprecatingly, and was half-indulgent towards, half-shocked by his master. The master-doll had his arm round the back of the man, and after a while this was how it seemed to the audience, that the doll was really the man because he was the manipulator and the man was really a doll, in spite of appearances, because he was sitting on the doll's knee. And indeed, when they got up and went out of the room, it was the man's legs that sagged.

The applause was half-hearted, spasmodic, slow, as if people were putting their hands together thoughtfully, not so as to show their appreciation.

Now came a man (or were there two men, or was it, in fact, a tiger? No, surely it couldn't be, it must be a man dressed in a tiger's skin) with a menacing sharp-toothed tiger head. The front man must be manipulating the head-piece which opened its jaws, head inclining to one side, as it roared out . . . instructions? The roaring sound must have been manipulated by the back legs (on a tape perhaps, it was so convincing) and one's only wish in the tensed audience was that the tiger would not discover one there, but would keep his attention on his girls. There were six girls, pathetic-looking, one got the impression they were doped. They were in spangles and tights in true circus fashion, but their skins were not made up so that they looked mottled, defenceless, unappealing. They followed each other in no sort of order to the acting area, where Karl had placed six cones in a circle. Five stood by their allotted cones, the sixth was unsure, she held back. The tiger approached slowly, commandingly, the ring of light, and his first roar startled out. The girls dropped to all-fours, but with no sort of precision. They looked as if they hadn't the sense to do what was expected of them, but that they were bound to do it all the same. Like a whip-crack the roar came again, as the tiger approached the girl out of place. She dropped to all fours, and as his fanged mouth opened in warning, she sped to her cone. Once more the roar rang out, and this time the girls climbed on to their cones. The same girl who had forgotten to stand by hers couldn't manage to mount her cone, it toppled, two other girls instinctively jumped down to go to her aid, but as the sharp warning roar came they jumped back to their places, leaving the unable one to confront her tormentor by herself.

He advanced upon her . . . the audience in the second and third rows stood up in terror, or perhaps merely not to miss the kill. There was a skirmish . . . the girl started to flee, but changed direction and again attempted to mount the cone, missed, and out of panic, in trying again, actually mounted it. The tiger turned with the pride of achievement to the audience. Karl shouted bravo! The audience followed suit.

Two men, incongruous by reason of their age, their cropped hair and their easily recognisable plain-clothes, walked purposefully towards Karl, quietly displaying their profession from inside their lapels. Karl bowed ironically.

'Twenty pence,' he said quietly, so as not to draw attention away from the act, and waited patiently to hand his blank sheets while the two men, unaccustomed to this approach, hunted uncomfortably in their pockets for change. But they didn't look at the sheets, for all they saw they might have been covered with programme notes.

Karl referred them to the wheel-chair. They turned towards her and repeated the ritual of the lapel. After a muttered colloquy she said out loud, 'Publicity!' and waved a red-taloned hand as dismissal of the subject. But not of them. She motioned them, with the same hand, graciously, to be seated. They complied, brows knit, perching themselves on the very edge of the kitchen chairs she had indicated. A ritual slow-motion march which had been going on meanwhile, continued. A pale drugged young man was lain across a small round table, such as might be found in any pub, his face and arms dangling over one side almost to the ground, the toe-caps of his shoes touching the floor on the other. The other performers began to chant, some in the manner of reciting psalms, others in the barking accents of military orders. They advanced slowly.

The audience could see nothing now but the backs of those actors nearest to them. The plain-clothes men rose slightly from their seats, uncertain . . . but the chanting stopped, and as the ritualists stepped back one sensed, though there was no sign of blood, no change in the position of the young man, that he was dead.

The old American woman smiled towards the plain-clothes and motioned them again to sit. Some of the ritualists left the acting area, giving the impression that their acting job for the night was over. One cleared his throat, another was already

146

unbuttoning his jacket, a third took an empty seat in the audience. Two of the others removed the young man, still in his
prostrate pose, as if he were a prop, and were followed by two
more carrying between them the table. It was over. There was
quiet applause.

But the old American woman in the wheel-chair with bright
red talon fingernails, was clapping her right hand against the
air ecstatically; it was only after a moment noticeable that she
had no left arm or hand to meet it to produce a sound.

It was at this moment that Ben appeared, naked 'unaccommodated man' in the doorway, just behind Ed. Ed turned
round but Ben seemed not to have noticed him. Like a busker
he started at once, his voice, a clear warning, 'Pray innocent,
and beware the foul fiend . . . Let but the herald cry, And . . .'

Karl shouted a military and peremptory 'Quiet!' Ben, surprised as an animal caught in the headlights' glare, stood still,
his words fading. In the silence Karl said to Ed, 'You're on
next.' Ed looked up. He had left the boy in the dressing-room,
not wanting to spoil the effect of velvet and lace before the
event.

'I'm fifth,' said Ed.

'You're on!' repeated Karl; he looked tensed and white. Ed,
feeling for the first time in his life what he supposed must ap-
proximate to stage-fright, rushed from the room, past the
puzzled Ben, to collect Tony. In the meantime Karl was on
the 'stage' and Ed could hear him 'I'm sorry . . . we have had to
cut the next act . . . As you'll see from your programmes (he
didn't seem to be fooling, many people glanced down at their
pieces of blank paper) it should have been . . .' his voice
faltered . . . amateurish . . . and trailed off . . . 'there's been an
accident.'

During the last part of his apology Ed was pushing Tony
forward to the piano. It can't have been easily discernible at
first whether Tony was a velvet-suited monkey, a freak, or a
boy; he walked with bandy legs, on the outer sides of his shoes

– he was merely uncomfortable, his clothes and shoes were too tight, but his walk to the piano was ambivalent. Ed waited on the side-lines; perhaps he looked like an anxious parent – or a trainer.

The boy mounted the stool and began. Short, simple pieces. After a while someone in the audience said, 'Oh, Christ,' and yawned loudly. 'Shut up!' said a girl. They were restless until gradually, as the virtuosity of the child became evident in the more elaborate pieces, they were held, motionless, all of them caught in the aura of the mystery of sound – sound without verbal meaning, momentous, all-pervading, true to the depths of each of them. Ed judged his time to be near, he caught Karl's wink, and shuffled in behind his props.

No one was disturbed. He came, ingratiatingly, to place the first one; then the second. Someone said 'ssh', perhaps it was Karl, someone else shushed him, concentration began to relax. Ed, holding in his impatience, deliberately placed nine, ten, eleven props, then losing control of his artistry, came suddenly downstage and with tremendous force hurled a chair, then the Venus, straight under the lid of the open piano. He was hot with fury. He kicked the stool from under the child, who, just as adamant, regained his balance and started playing standing up.

The audience yelled, most of them in furious pity at the interruption, a few of the women because of compassion for the child, and some of them with the primitive urge to destroy, which Ed had released. He no longer had the props to himself, people were rushing at them, hurling them at each other, at the piano, at the child. The jumble of shouts and words and noises reached a deafening crescendo when Ed could no longer contain his excitement. He fired the shot. The child slumped across the keys, which let out a feeble mew.

The old woman was clawing with her one hand, the nails seeming to drip blood into the air, fluttering a million-dollar bill as if it would pay for Armageddon. 'Kill! Kill!' she yelled. 'Kill! Kill!' until someone (it was possibly a c.i.d. man) obeyed her, and shot, first of all the grasping hand, and then the shouting mouth. Karl had rushed to the adjoining room where the artists were in different stages of undress, their faces smeared with grease and greasepaint. 'On stage everyone,' he yelled, 'don't stop and dress, come!'

Frightened, bare-armed, bare-legged, in sad unattractive underwear, they obeyed. He drove them into the hall before him, and squeezing in himself, he turned and locked the door. There were already many dead. The artists stood shocked, uncertain whether they had been called to stop the massacre, to join in, or merely to watch. Before they had time to catch the bloodbath infection they were cudgelled, trampled on, or lynched.

The air was stifling, foetid. Ed, still mad with the lust of total completion, his heart pumping fiendishly with the effort of lifting and throwing huge unwieldy objects, felt suddenly a constriction in his breast. His muscles were still able, flexed, his body and will more powerful than he had ever known them were rejoicing in the action, but his irritated lungs eventually drew his brain's attention to their distress. The signal was not that his body was giving out, it was that something outside him was amiss; and like a horse in panic his nostrils located it.

It was the stench of burning. The smoke that had gradually been enveloping him, shading the dead and dying bodies from his eyes, was not an imaginative screening, but a thickening reality. The shutters, as his hands reached up to unlock them, were scorching hot, the wood already buckling so that the iron bolts could not be released even had he been able to hold them. He made, animal-like, for the doors, stumbled unseeing over piled bodies, reached it with the last strength of his bursting lungs; and found it locked. He turned to look at the scene of his will. It was aflame. Not for a moment had he ever imagined that he too would be destroyed in a holocaust.

He had seen himself rather as a painter depicting a scene, outside the horrendous canvas. His destructive thrill gave way to a terrified yell of outrage. 'Not me!' he gasped. 'Not me! Them! You! Them! Not me! Not me!' His scorched brain succumbed to the agony, was fiercely, crackingly gorged in the tongue and then the sheet of fire.

Ben shrieked:

'Men must endure
Their going hence, even as their coming hither,'
and suddenly, weakly, his strength spent in the effort to be heard, hanging his head,

'Poor Tom's a-cold.'
But poor Tom, naked though he was, was not left cold for long. The long tongue of flame darted at him, licked, skinned and blistered him, together with those who had heeded him and those who had not. In the charred silence that followed, from the place where the piano had stood, came notes of their own accord, sighing into the air.

Jes - u   Joy of man's desiring

No one was alive to hear. The sound tinkled, pure and simple, into the empty dawn.

'Wake up Chris!'

He couldn't place who she was, nor where he was, in a rational perspective; because rationality and perspective had gone, had lost their meaning. He fought his mind back to the time when such things had been, and remembered first of all a filmed-over mind-picture of Claire moulding a piece of plasticine between her fingers. Another dim film of picture, under-exposed, flipped up in his mind – a picture of the steps of Eros, and himself on them, vaguely searching, scanning the faces in the grey wetness of a Piccadilly Circus whose lights failed to illumine the beings huddled there.

'Chris!'

The voice was high and thin; and he knew his name as a label he could not deny.

He knew from the tone of voice that he would be forced to 'come to' to revisit a world in which he himself had no part. He saw his pyjama-legs, his bony feet and ankles sticking out from them; he'd done without them, or without consciousness of them for so long that he wondered now why he had to take them along with him. He turned his head away from them, away from the girl, pulled a pillow over his face, and tried to re-enact limbo. He had no desire to go further back, to what lay before that; that confused life was away from him now, lying translated into type and scratched out type, on paper.

Where? He sat up quickly, saw the pile of paper there on the floor, and relieved, hid his head again under the softness.

Lying there, allowing himself to re-enter his thoughts, he decided he was cold, and that his left shoulder ached. And also that he was hungry. He sat up quickly. 'Coffee!' he commanded, 'and toast.' 'The toaster's broken,' she said. 'Bread then, and butter.'

His own life, after all, had its compensations. Food for one. Toast (or bread), coffee. It was like convalescence, being waited on.

He lay back, basking in the delicious emptiness of waiting for food, between two worlds into neither of which need he commit himself. He let her sugar his coffee when she came admiring her slender fingers and the delicate nostrils of her rather long nose.

He grinned at her. Looking past her and on to the floor, his mouth full of bread, he took a sudden revulsion to the wadge of

paper lying there – paper of different sizes, even odd envelopes and wrapping paper, used when he'd foolishly forgotten to stock up for a Sunday. It looked defenceless without
a folder – pathetic – second-hand even now, the morning
after he had finished it; finished with it.

How could he have become so involved? So certain that it
had to be done? The whole concept was so puerile looked at
with hindsight, that he wanted nothing more to do with it; it
was embarrassing. How had he been living during these last
months? Had he gone about bragging, when he wasn't
actually committing the nonsense to paper, 'I'm writing a
novel . . . I'm busy . . . I'm doing something?'

He hoped he hadn't done anything so shaming – should he
ask her? Or wouldn't she have noticed, or remembered? He
got up, dressed (it was Sunday he discovered, and already
three o'clock in the afternoon) and as the convalescent day
passed, he remembered, little by little, about her, and about
himself. His parents already knew her, didn't they? Yes – he
seemed to remember that his parents had reluctantly accepted his way of life – remembered his mother saying of her,
'I like her, dear.'

He looked out of the window on to peeling, porticoed
houses – where the hell was this place? Was he in Islington?
North London? Shepherd's Bush? Camberwell? South Ken?

'Don't tell me,' he said. 'I want to guess where we are.'

'Lucky I'm used to you,' she replied, 'or I'd think you were
bonkers. Anyway,' she stroked his hand firmly with a finger,
as if he were a marble surface, 'congratulations on finishing
it.'

He shrugged. 'It's dreadful,' he said quietly, well aware
now that whatever other qualities or defects she had, he was
able to confide in her.

'You always say that.'

So . . . he wasn't a braggart then? So much the better; it
would have been painful to climb down from any conceit he

might have shown during the last months. So . . . even when he'd been most absorbed, most happy in his work, when he'd felt, during those rare moments, that all was going well, he hadn't been fool enough to say so out loud in this other, stranger, but strangely emptier world.

Straining his ears, he thought he heard a train breathing out, in a relaxed stationary mood; but it might have been his inner ear listening to his own rhythm. He decided, while she prepared the lunch in the passage outside, that he would not be curious, would ask no questions, would let things unfold themselves to him gradually, or in spurts of cognition, just as he had when he was writing. Soon, this porticoed life would take over, become more real than Ed and his attitudes – at the moment it was hidden, empty, without energy. Well, that other life was dead too now as far as he was concerned, and might never be resuscitated. He himself had no desire to go back and live it; standing aside from it, seeing it now not as the throbbing pulse of his life but as a pile of limp typescript, he could not even mourn it; not only did it seem to him worthless, but it had nothing whatever to do with himself. He felt ashamed.

I can't write, never will. This is not it; I am not one of them . . . I am a wretched ungifted mediocrity. Then, if I am just that, what am I doing alive? What can I do to justify the fact that that wretched ungifted mediocrity of a man spawned me on to a ditto ditto ditto of a woman . . . because even *that* needs a sort of justification. I have been vouchsafed breathing apparatus – what am I going to do about it? Pass the time? While it away . . . in despair? Are others, all others, in despair, too? Then why do they hide it? For the same reason that I do: that they are too cowardly to face it?

He was inordinately lazy, he never wanted to create again; he'd rather sleep and let things happen . . . or let nothing happen. He took only the feeblest interest in life. Sex had no urgency, it was as if he were performing it for someone else, he

153

didn't even bother to disguise the fact. He was surprised that she stayed on. He had forgotten that she too was absorbed in her work. In the middle of the room he now saw what looked like a head shrouded in a cloth. He lifted a corner of the wet linen and found below a lump of clay that bore a frightening resemblance to someone he knew . . . yes, it was, it was himself . . . an unfinished, muddy, indeterminate blotch; and placed on a pedestal too, as if it had importance. Odd, she was probably being absorbed in her effigy while he was being absorbed somewhere else. She wouldn't have missed him; she was creating her own idea of him, hadn't really needed him there all those weeks? months? except as a model, a reference, for her own idea of him. He felt a tinge of self-pity. What had he expected of her?

That she would be waiting on *his* side lines until he returned to their shared world? But why should he have wanted her around, when he himself was somewhere else? He couldn't complain of her, she was here ready to make him coffee, to leave her imaginary world when he woke from his, enquire into his, feed him, respond to him.

'I want the best of both worlds,' he said aloud, and wondered why he had previously not asked himself what that could mean.

For the next few days he let her look after him – let himself lie in bed as he had at his mother's house, watched her manipulate with her strong fingers, the primitive substance, noted only half-consciously that she didn't even look towards him, but was intent on her creation – her mouth firmly fixed, lines embedded at the corners. But as the head developed more to her liking she made verbal contact with him when she brought the food to his bedside; and finally, when she reached a level of satisfaction with her work, and felt freed enough to think of his, 'Are you going to write another book?' He gazed at her.

'After *that* abortive mess? I'm going back to studying rock formation, stones – like I did as a child; it was more restful, and I liked it. I don't like writing.'

'Stones are beautifully static,' she said, 'and rocks.'

'They're stable,' he agreed. 'Restful; they don't get out of hand.'

'And they're so inhuman.'

'Yes!' he agreed delightedly. 'Yes! And what's more they don't die.'

'They don't live, either,' she said thoughtfully, 'but at least they exist.'

But remorse for the book kept him awake at night. The thing that appalled about creative writing was that he, Chris, didn't have to live it – to *be* it – to feel it – only, like an armchair general, survey it on paper; while in the trenches of his imagination people were being burnt alive; and not only for the space of a few pages, but for eternity. If he condemned them to burn, or worse, neglected to put out the fire because of ineptitude, they were condemned to the pain, with no redress. Yes, yes, a blank was preferable. But was it? Once confronted with the blank, one began to see the possibilities inherent in creation. There at least were the possibilities of love, of beauty, of talent, of an understanding between beings. In blankness, nothing was possible. Was one crowded hour of painful life worth an age without a name? Anyway he had no choice. He had created, and now abandoned. They were doomed to the existence he had thought up for them; and he could not now change them. But had he, perhaps, even unwittingly, left their minds to imagine with as they wished? Could they not get out of their inhibiting skins through a flight of mind? But what of Tony and his like? He, his author, had specifically given him a limited mind – how could such a mind fly? But it did didn't it? Despite Chris's decree, Tony's mind of its own volition flew to heights of musicality that his creator had never reached nor would ever understand, or even try to.

On the 7th day he slept.

Glaring faults he hadn't noticed before. Was it too late to change them? He told himself it was, out of laziness, and because he no longer cared. Inconsistencies, omissions, feeblenesses, crudities – oh well it was the best he could do (was it?) and it was done. Looked at as a whole Eva was both alive and dead simultaneously. It was only if you started at the beginning for the first time that you didn't realise that. He knew now; they were all playing their entrances and exits concurrently. If he should ever wake up to wish himself a second chance, which word would he begin with? How to begin with a word without first thinking of a letter? Or a number? But what word would do if there was no concept. That was it – he must begin with a concept – where were they kept? How should he look for one? In stillness? In the dark? Certainly searching would lead nowhere, as there was nothing anywhere to find. He must invent. He must be the Prime Mover. No, not mover, there was nothing to move. Or was there? Was that a definition of still darkness, that it was moveable. Move yes. He shifted his legs in bed. No, not body move. Mind. Move your mind. Mind your next move. How did he know he had a second chance anyway? He didn't but he was going to chance it. Chance his arm. No, not arm, mind. Mind! Care! Yes, he must care. Care more this time. Care for. Take care of.

'The spirits, bodiless, each his own god . . .' no; 'the bodies, spiritless, crude matter . . .' no. Perhaps the thing to do was to write the second paragraph first, then there'd be no need for the difficulty of beginning. And autobiographically; so that there'd be no need for thought, only for remembrance. In this way the lifelessness of himself and the people around

156

him might be imbued with some essence of a palpable reality.

'The boys who hurtled, thick knee'd or sharp-knee'd out of the door and across the asphalt playground were . . .' 'The mother was tiny, her eyebrows . . .' words were inelegant – useless . . . he didn't want them; what he wanted was to break the bounds of dictionary-imprisoned letters, to write a book out of mind-stuff. It could be done . . . composers did it; they didn't have to make sense . . . yet even they were confined to one element, the sound universe. Why should he not express the whole of vibrating life by mixing sound and written word, numbers and paint. . . . Ben would say with a grin 'We do that in the theatre' . . . but the theatre was an outworn mode of expression, fit for children to perform and to watch; no not children, but adults arrested in their development who had remained childish. He'd start off with a typewriter . . . convey bits (but bits of what, and what bits?) on to paper, and then . . . ? To start creating, even re-creating, meant starting from nothing, not jumping to conclusions. To start meant emptying oneself of all preconception. Inert, he lay in a self-induced coma which barred entry, or rather admitted everything to the threshold, and then turned each and everything away. What persisted was day and night. Light and darkness. He let them enter. They seemed good. Aeons (was it?) later, he allowed entry to salt water and rock, fresh water and desert. He lay content, and slept.

When he woke a migraine danced behind his eyelids. 'Liver,' his mother would have said. The dots split and danced anew, split again, until his head felt as if it would burst with the pain. His eyes watered and the dots swam in it . . . when would they finish? They were clawing at his eyes now, growing larger and larger . . . to the size of Brontosauruses. The smaller ones flew up . . . all were out of his grasp, unwieldly . . . oh well, couldn't be helped, he was too tired to bother; let them get on with it. The mistakes would have to put up with themselves.

She brought him science fiction from the library and geographic magazines. He pored over them – but nothing met his need, and he had to admit to himself that he needed nothing. One day, in case she should leave him, he said, 'I've been like this before – but I get over it.'

She said, 'I said we'd go over to Ben and Cis this evening . . .'

No inkling of surprise troubled him. 'Fine,' he said. He looked forward to it. For the first time he was eager to know where he was. He held in his impatience, trying like a kidnapped man to guess where he was by sound, by the minute indications that separate one district from another. Being another Sunday (Claire had said so) it was too difficult. He heard a man's voice, pitched sharply, hurl emphatically what must have been an insult, in a language he couldn't identify. The window of their room gave on to this road of porticoed uniform plaster-peeled house fronts, with steps leading up to the front doors; few of which windows were curtained. An overturned and neglected tricycle lay on the pavement opposite.

They walked dusty streets to a bus stop. 'W.2.' he read. Paddington? Possibly. The bus ride was delicious well-being. He put his arm round her. They didn't speak.

A flight of iron stairs and a passage lead to an unlit corridor. Suddenly his legs felt heavy with water, the rest of his body void. He was aware of a racing pulse in his temple. Then blood rushed in painfully as in a thaw.

'Hallo,' Claire knocked with her chunky silver snake-headed ring . . . 'can we come in?'

The female voice inside had stopped mid-sentence. The door opened. Ben was wearing a thick white sweater over blue cotton denims – he was barefoot; there was no mistaking his smile . . . he welcomed them delightedly, without preliminaries, racing at once into a description of what had happened at a rehearsal. He was not showing off, he himself had not been involved in the story; it was his exuberance, not the incident itself, that laid the way for the pleasant warmth of a friendly evening.

Chris's blood settled to normal temperature. Perhaps, after all . . .

Cis had not spoken, had hardly looked up in greeting, but had immediately started unscrewing the top of one beer-bottle, and filling their glasses. Relaxed now, happy, pleased to be back, Chris asked, 'How are the kids?' as she proffered him his glass.

'What kids?'

Her wary eyes flickered in hesitation, then she shrugged. 'I never understand your jokes,' she said .'Sorry.'

She switched on the portable radio on the table, and began buttering some bread for the sandwiches.

'I'll help you,' he said. He felt contrite. It was more than likely that she couldn't have children, or that she'd had a miscarriage or that Ben was impotent. Or that she'd recently had an abortion? He knew nothing about this tight, thin-lipped girl; why had he ventured to ask her anything? He decided not to speak again but to show by actions that he wished to be friendly.

The radio was playing Haydn, or rather, as Chris reminded himself, people were playing Haydn somewhere; and the valves in the radio had picked it up; or more likely still an orchestra had once played Haydn (in sections) in a recording studio, for a disc, and some girl in the b.b.c. or o.r.t.f. or whatever was putting the disc on a turntable.

He busied himself putting cheese and chutney on to her buttered bread; the beer as usual made him want the lavatory almost as soon as he'd drunk it. He left the room, without hesitation found the closet, and on his way back glanced up the few steps of the room where . . . should he go and look?

Might there be someone there? He could hardly pretend he'd mistaken the room – neither Ben nor Cis would believe

159

him anyway. He stood in indecision. He knew, of course, what he would *not* find, what intrigued him was what he *would*. He decided to ask Ben – he didn't want to disconcert Cis again . . . he would wait till later in the evening, and find a convenient opportunity, when no one would be put out by his question. He had plenty of time to work out how to frame such a question so as least to embarrass himself and them.

He went back into their room, and got caught up in the shallow, uninhibited talk. Claire, he discovered, was more intelligent than he was; why had he assumed that she was not? Were there really still echoes inside him of his father's assumption that everyone he met, especially women, must of necessity be beneath him in acumen, astuteness, or whatever it was his father (and please heaven not himself) prided himself on? At the thought of his father, who had hardly entered his mind for months, he decided he'd like to see his parents again; something like affection, but not so warm, tinged his memory of them. Was it perhaps compassion; had he at last grown up enough to see them as other people saw them, pathetic perhaps but not beneath contempt?

To his surprise Ben was talking about a black actor friend who . . . and here Chris dragged himself quickly back to the present . . . had once rented the room at the top of those stairs.

'He said it was haunted, so he left. So did Jean – do you remember, Cis? But we thought she was potty anyway so we took no notice. We've advertised . . . we don't need it. Like it, Claire?'

'In what way haunted?' she asked.

Chris was amazed that he didn't have to lead the conversation; it was happening as if willed by him.

'It wasn't haunted,' Cis said. She was very definite.

'Well,' Ben admitted, 'we have heard sounds.'

'*You* have,' she corrected. 'I haven't. And anyway your imagination always runs away with you. If neither Gary nor Jean had said anything, you wouldn't have noticed.'

'That's true,' Ben agreed, 'it's probably my inventive mind.'

'What sort of sounds?' Chris spoke for the first time; his throat constricted.

'Not sounds exactly,' Ben admitted, 'but as if something is falling – more of a sensation really.'

Chris stood up. It would be easy now to say 'Let's go and look'. The way was paved, as if intentionally. He heard himself say instead, 'May I help myself to some more beer?' as if he were a middle-aged bourgeois member of a golf or cricket club visiting a crony. The moment passed, the conversation slipped easily into the theory of acoustics – the Chichester Theatre – wood as a sounding board – water – in which Chris joined with zest and pleasure. The fact was, he really did not want to know about that room. The threshold might be too difficult and too unpleasant to cross.

Ben said, 'What happened to that book you were writing?'

'That what?'

'That book you . . .'

'Oh, that. I left it on the floor. Months ago.'

'Why don't you get it published?'

'It's not good enough.'

'You've tried?'

'No.'

'Then you don't know. Why haven't you?'

'I tried to try . . . I answered a couple of phoney ads.'

'I know a literary agent . . . chap who was in a play with me once – terrible actor. Gave it up and does extremely well now. Want me to mention you to him?'

'Not really.'

'Why not?'

'Well,' Chris admitted, truthfully for a change, 'if I don't send it to anyone I can go on thinking it's an unknown masterpiece.'

'What good does *that* do your ego?'

G.I.I.—F

'I don't know,' he said lamely. 'I think I'm frightened of failure.'

'But you're living with it now.'

'So I am, so I am.'

'So what's wrong with it when you've already got it?'

Chris grinned. 'I'd like to meet him,' he said, though he felt cold with premonition.

The following week he gave Ben the typescript to read – happy at the delay before showing it to the agent: 'I've only got the one copy.'

He got a job as a waiter and endeavoured to wake himself up by pretending to be different nationalities, at the same time as leaving himself asleep by skimming shallowly, skin-deep over the people he was pretending to be. Playing at it. He became, superficially, a Cypriot, a Spaniard, a Hungarian. This last was his favourite, he simply could *not* understand a word the customers said, and would delightedly bring them a roll and butter when they asked for a bill, or an ice-cream if they asked for soup. For a few days he was a Pakistani (with the help of Ben's make-up) but he didn't enjoy cleaning his face and hands afterwards, so he soon gave it up. Once in an unguarded moment, when he was a 'resting' American pop-singer 'doing' Europe, he suddenly got a signal-like flash for a new book. 'Down Fido!' he yelled, and nearly dropped his tray. One of the two women he was serving did him the honour of looking down for the dog. 'Did you get bitten?' she asked, perplexed. 'You can say that again,' he answered in his best Southern States drawl. She took him literally and repeated her question. He lowered his lids and lugged chewing-gum from one side of his mouth to the other.

He confided in Ben, 'I didn't want to kill her, or the child, why should I want to kill the innocent? But things got out of hand,

and Ed got too strong – and then Karl, whom I hadn't reckoned on at all – he was just a deaf man in a mac at first – pulled
the strings, and that American woman . . . I stopped being
able to control them. Of course I could have just stopped
writing, but I didn't think of it, and anyway I didn't want to.
I wanted to see what they did.' He added, surprisingly un-
ashamed of his failure, 'I suppose for a bit I really thought
they existed.'

'You can't draw a line,' Ben said, 'between reality and un-
reality. It's subjective. And just because you put someone you
knew into a book . . .'

Chris opened his eyes wide. 'Did I know you before . . . ?'

'Christ Almighty,' said Ben compassionately, 'did you think
the chicken came before the egg?'

'Yes, I thought you were in the book first.'

'No, old love, we existed before. Claire introduced you to
us; she was at school with Cis, remember? Not that it makes
any difference . . .'

'And the room upstairs?'

'What about it?'

'Did I ever go into it?'

'Did you? *I* don't know. Could've. It was full of magazines and dustbin lids before we let it . . .'

'Yes it was,' said Chris. 'Yes it was.'

'The differences as I see them,' he was eager to talk about
what worried him most, 'are pain and time. In reality pain is
continuous, in imagination pain can be put down and picked
up again.'

'I suggest,' said Ben, 'that Edgar is more alive than I am.'

'Edgar? Who's Edgar?'

'In *Lear*.'

'You're not still in that?'

'Never was.'

'Oh, no, sorry . . . I was . . .'

'Edgar,' said Ben, brushing the mistake aside as an irrelev-

163

ance, 'is more alive than I am, partly if you like because he suffered more than I.'

'No! That's what I'm saying,' said Chris, 'he didn't suffer at all.'

'But partly because,' Ben accepted the interruption but pursued his own line of thought, 'partly because the mind that made him was, I suspect, richer than the mind that made me.'

'Heh! Heh! That's a quibble; the mind that made you made the mind that made Edgar.'

'Ah!' said Ben, 'there's the rub. The mind may have made Shakespeare's embryonic mind, but what that made mind made of itself was entirely within its own power.'

'Could I,' asked Chris, 'have – superstitiously or any other way – through my mind, however feeble, through a sort of voodoo if you like, hurt you physically – I mean like sticking in pins or whatever . . .'

'You mean might I die in a fire because you imagined it?'

'Yes.'

'Doubtful,' said Ben. 'I should say you're suffering from hubris and the gods have a way of punishing that particular vice – you'll probably go potty.'

'Well, the god of evolution must by definition be potty mustn't he?'

'No . . . only inexperienced,' said Ben. 'He makes mistakes . . .'

Chris tapped on the glass partition. It didn't open from his side. The girl and woman inside took no notice, went on chatting in what looked like a desultory manner. He tapped again. The younger one glanced in his direction and away again, her conversation seeming to grow more animated. He pulled faces; stuck his thumbs in his cheeks and pulled down the skin

164

under his eyes with his middle fingers as he had done in the mirror every evening between six and nine years old, to the accompaniment of his mother's pale remonstrance. 'Chris – you'll stay like that.' This was, in fact, the challenge: he dared himself to stay like that for life, visualised himself as an old man selling matches, drooping red under-lids and hunched up cheeks, thumbs and middle fingers no longer necessary to keep the face in place, free to hold the tray of proffered matches. 'Only four pence a bunch,' he moaned, through the partition – it sounded like only four fence a frunch, which he knew they'd have found amusing if only they could hear. Behind him a man with an umbrella passed, and opening the door four paces along the passage, went into the room. Why couldn't they have told him there was a door for Christ's sake, or at least indicated that it was there with a head-nod. The man had shut the door, was miming speech with the girl.

Chris pulled his jacket over his head so that he looked like a hunchback in a storm and trotted to open the door. Inside he stood with dangling arms and waited. See who speaks first. The girl wouldn't; it was the older woman who eventually, irritably, said, 'Yes?'

'I want to thee Mithter Townley.'

'He's out,' she said.

'He's *out*,' the girl corroborated, raising her voice as if lispers and long arms must automatically be hard of hearing. Chris grabbed victory quickly – it was always an elusive state; he put his jacket back to its usual and more comfortable place and said in a haughty deep-toned voice, 'Oh no he's not – he has a luncheon appointment with me.'

They left him alone for a few minutes, dealt with the other man who had come to pick up a parcel, talked to each other about the time, about where they would lunch; then the girl slowly, indifferently picked up the telephone and said, 'Your lunch date Mr Townley.'

165

Chris rifled through some magazines, re-assuming the persona of a young author meeting an agent to discuss his first book.

'Hallo there!' Mr Townley was brusque, bluff, business-like, a veritable b . . . of a man.

Chris lost confidence at once. Somehow he had expected a man who had been an actor to be more like Ben, small, warm, young. This man was tall, middle-aged, had a neat moustache, and was dressed in a blue city suit. It was unnerving.

'Well now!' was what Mr Townley said next. They shook hands, and walked out on to the pavement. Chris hoped the girl had noticed that he hadn't noticed her as he left.

'I've booked a table at the Frayère, o.k.?'

'Fine,' muttered Chris, as if it wasn't the place he would have chosen himself, but would do well enough. Not that he'd ever heard of the Frayère; but as the agent's office was in Soho, he supposed that the restaurant would be too.

The Spanish . . . Greek . . . Cypriot . . . or Ukranian . . . maître d'hôtel showed them to their table with a long arm outstretched and a head indication.

'Monsieur Townley,' he said in greeting. 'Monsieur Townley' was obviously known here, this was 'his' table; where he entertained clients; penniless ones like himself? Chris wondered, or famous ones who knew how to behave, how to choose from a menu, knew that 'What'll you have?' meant 'What'll you drink?'

'I'm easy' was all Chris could say to any question about what he'd have either to eat or drink, when in fact he was feeling less easy than he could ever remember having been. It was no good telling himself that this was the classic situation from Dickens to Osborne, it didn't help. His feet were sweating and he had a great desire to scratch his head, not just in one place, but all over, as if there were nits there. He took out a comb nonchalantly and stabbed them to death, meanwhile studying the menu which was confusing, not only by being in two languages, but by being written long-hand and roneo'd.

'You'd think they could afford a typist.' No, he wouldn't say it out loud, after all the Monsieur was paying for him. He surreptitiously pointed the comb on its way back to his pocket, at the menu, whatever it pointed to he'd have. To his relief it was something he understood.

'Mixed grill,' he said, 'I'll have mixed grill,' and yawned as if the very thought of it bored him.

'And what for starters?' Good God, did they really stuff like Henry VIII when they got into the money? He looked at the dish written one above, 'Osso Bucco,' he said, 'I'll have a little Osso Bucco for a change.' Bucking bronco? Oh well, if it was horse meat that was their fault for putting it on the menu.

'Really?' said Mr Townley. He sounded genuinely surprised. 'No, only my fun,' said Chris; he hadn't fancied horse meat anyway. 'What are you starting with?' Why hadn't he thought of this gambit before?

'Melon, I think, or possibly Terrine . . .' 'Melon?' Chris seemed to be savouring the idea, 'no I don't *think* so . . . Terrine I should say.' 'Right,' said Mr Townley amicably, 'we'll have Terrine.'

The choosing of food and wine, the tasting of it, and the chat about it was so absorbing that Chris quite forgot that he was out for anything more than a school treat with a rich uncle. Not that he'd ever had an uncle, rich or poor, but he recognised the situation none the less. When the dessert came 'Yeah, I'll have some of those green figs . . . yeah all right, some chocolate cake with it,' (the waiter's suggestion, pointing to the laden trolley), 'O.k. some cream, yes . . .' he had a sudden feeling that they'd be saying goodbye soon, and nothing about the business in hand would have been approached.

In fact, after food talk they had covered a fair range of subjects none of them particularly appealing to Chris: car park-

167

ing problems; taxation; the state of international football; where to buy the best men's shoes ('I have peculiar feet,' Mr Townley confided in him); and Chris, with the plate of cake and fruit in front of him, decided to plunge. 'Well, here goes . . .' he began.

Mr Townley held up a hand to a passing waiter and raising his eyebrows at Chris. 'Coffee?' They ordered coffee. 'Bring it now,' Mr Townley ordered. 'Sorry,' he said to Chris, 'but I have an appointment at 3.30 and time's a little short.'

'Well,' Chris plunged again. 'What did you think of it?'

'Of what?'

'The Book.'

'Oh, I haven't read it myself, don't have time.' In spite of its fullness, Chris's stomach felt weak and empty; he was lost, didn't know where to go from here. He spooned a pippy fig into his mouth.

'I've had a reader's report – not too promising – but we might see what we can do.'

'It's o.k. I can take it somewhere else . . .'

'No, no, leave it with us for a few months, I'll send it around, you never know . . . ah, coffee?'

Chris practised future skin-preserving, face-saving conversations; though his skin felt so thin that a tiny pin-scratch would have bled him to death, and his face was burning with a mixture of shame at his own naïveté, and sudden hatred of Mr Townley's moustache, and the moles on the back of his hand which was now signing a bill.

('What happened to that book of yours?'

'Oh, that? It's with an agent at the moment actually.'

'Any luck?'

'Well, I gather a number of publishing firms are interested, he's trying to get the best price.')

Months?

'How long does a publisher take to say yes or no?' He didn't want to hide behind trickery and ambiguity any longer, he wanted to ask a straight question and get a straight answer.

'Some take six weeks, eight weeks, a little longer . . . depends.'

Mr Townley looked at his watch, he had finished his coffee, and already had his palms on the side of the table, ready to push it away from his chair and get up.

'And how many publishers (on average) before a book is accepted. Usually, I mean?'

He saw the stupidity of the question before he had finished it.

Mr Townley grinned. 'You don't want to get too depressed until round about the nineteenth,' he said. 'Then I think we call it a day.'

Why can't I do mental arithmetic, six weeks times nineteen equals not quite as much as 120 – but there are only 52 weeks in a year! . . . 'Hey! Wait a minute,' he said belligerently, meaning both 'wait while I take in the import of what you've said,' and also 'don't push that table at me, I haven't finished my coffee.'

He had nothing, nothing to lose now, so he may as well ask it, 'And how long, *after* it's accepted, *if*, I mean only *if* it's ever taken, before it's in print, and in a shop?' After all his Mum and Dad might want to buy one if they weren't either in their dotage or their graves by then.

'Oh, nine months to a year, can be less; could be six months, I really must go. Good luck.'

The old man with drooping underlids was no longer a childhood glimpse into a macabre future, it was here, now, himself. The book sat on a counter in a shop and he was outside selling matches, his beard scraping the top of his dirty toecaps . . . He was dossing under newspaper on a bench in a square, ignored by Shakespeare above, whose pate was being used as a lavatory seat by pigeons . . . He left the restaurant hunched up, but no longer in mockery of himself or anyone else. He walked along the Soho pavement, and didn't even greet the photographed huge nude bosoms and bellies that were pasted outside the strip-tease clubs. His sense of the ridiculous had deserted him. He only wanted to be sick.

What, after all, did it amount to, what did it contribute to the sum of things – was not a non-creative void, a sleep, a death, preferable to this unacceptable mess where men shot children and the public applauded? How had he conceived of anything so banal? Well, it wasn't his fault really, why should authors be expected to be oracles, to create things as the characters would have wished. Gone were the times when one could create heroes and heroines all striving towards a perfection, a one-ness, a well-being with their creator. The truth was he simply couldn't be bothered any more, and furthermore, he didn't think anyone wanted him to be bothered.

Somewhere, past his pin-prick, outside time and space as he knew it, other gods were 'having a go' – but he was too tired to make the effort to find out what they were doing. He'd simply go to sleep. He didn't at this moment reckon on waking up – but . . . perhaps . . . when he'd slept out his nausea . . .

He had taken it for granted that anything mortal began in embryo, that the sequence was small at birth and, given a life-span, larger at death . . . that flowers, fruit, men and their imaginative creations all began with a seed and developed gradually, sometimes imperceptibly to a ripeness, decaying perhaps towards the end . . . But could not whole other universes (as most certainly could the creative imagination of man) arrive fully ripened and descend towards babyhood, womb-hood and death? Could there not be worlds, as in his own mind, that started with unimportant, superficial details, and enriched themselves as they grew? From the outside inwards, rather than inside out? And what of coincidence? Accident? The unforeseen? Ben was even now on an Arts Council tour of the smaller towns of England, Scotland and Wales, playing Edgar in *King Lear*. Voodoo? Logical sequence? Wish-fulfilment? Prescience? Accident? Coincidence? Plan? A mistake in time?

'Can I speak to Mr Townley?' He didn't mock himself or the girl who answered, he wasn't in the mood.

'Hello! Yes, Chris!' all cheery . . . 'no, no point in letting you know about rejections old boy . . . we'll let you know if there's any good news . . .'

He dared: 'Could I see the rejections? I mean, could you let me know?'

'Sorry, old boy, haven't the time or the staff. Must rush now.'

'But I *collect* them,' Chris said to himself in the smelly phone booth. 'I *collect* rejection slips. I've got a scrapbook all ready for them. It's my *hobby*.'

It was like standing for forty minutes for the right number bus . . . if *no bus* at all came along one was in despair, but as the wrong numbers loomed up in the distance – the tiny message of hope that soon one would be warm and comfortable and on one's way, was what kept one standing there against all odds. *Hope.* But if he wasn't even going to be told when the wrong buses came up – then he'd stand alone here facing a long blank street in which no lighted false red hope would ever raise his spirits.

'Who is it please?'

'Sorry, he's out.'

'What name? Mr Townley is at a meeting.'

'Who's speaking? He's away for the week.'

'Sorry, he's out.'

'*Out.*'

Yours sincerely, and then a squiggle that might have been de-ciphered as Cerey or Arham. Chris who had covered the letter with his left hand, now shifted his hand downwards to expose the address. Dean Street. Cerey was not Arham but Oscar, or on looking closer, more persistently, was more likely to be Oscar

Townley. He lay on his back in bed. Claire having tactfully tossed him the envelope had gone to make the coffee for breakfast. It was now two years and three weeks since he had first met Townley. Chris rehearsed, out of a superstition that what he could imagine would not come to pass, the communications he would least like to receive. 'Dear Chris, after all this time I feel we must dissociate ourselves from your unpublishable book.' Or 'Dear Sir, since we have now sent the book to 37 publishers, all of whom have declined it (some rudely), we feel it is now time to despatch same back to you.' Or 'Dear Sir, we need all our shelves for publishable manuscripts. If you don't remove your rubbish within 24 hours we shall assume you want us to chuck it into the dustbin.'

His curiosity could wait no longer. He took away his hand and read:

Dear Chris,

As you can see from the following list we have now sent your book to the following publishers:

Hodder and Stoughton	Hutchinson
Gollancz	Blond and Briggs
Heinemann	Longmans
Collins	Blackies
Eyre and Spottiswoode	André Deutsch
Chatto and Windus	Bodley Head
Faber and Faber	George Weidenfeld
Hamish Hamilton	W. H. Allen
Arthur Barker	Macmillans
Putnams	Michael Joseph

all of whom have turned it down.

I have today managed to get a small but reputable firm, Martin and Nightingale, to accept it. They were not at first keen, but I spoke to one of their managing directors on the phone and finally persuaded him, for an advance of £50, to take it. The fee is not high, but I fear beggars can't be choosers.

Yours sincerely,

[Sgd] Squiggle

Chris's mind and body had trouble in deciding whether to be elated or depressed. Elation won. He leapt out of bed, crowed, did mock gymnastic exercises, goose-stepped, and finally, as Claire came towards him with the coffee-pot, rushed at her in an attempt to hug her, scalding both of them. She dropped the pot and the contents poured over their bare feet. His triumph subsided with the pain, and his only recourse was to blame her. 'Once in a lifetime, once in a lifetime, I have a piece of good news, and what happens, all you can do is complain about your burnt stomach and your blistered feet.'

But he was in pain too, and found it difficult to keep up his enthusiasm with his toes smarting. She filled the washing-up bowl with cold water, and one by one they plunged their four feet into it. As she threw him a towel he said, 'Fifty rotten pounds; for a year's work and two years and three weeks of waiting. Fifty measly pounds. No, forty-five – he takes ten per cent.'

'It's been accepted?' Her eyes lit with pleasure, her voice scaled upwards. 'Chris? Has it?'

'Yes,' he said, trying to sound still depressed, 'but read the letter; it's sickening.'

She laughed. 'Accepted! You're an author!'

'I'm no more an author now than I was yesterday.' He wanted her to show him how thrilled he should be, wanted her to voice his delight, but felt the need to decry it himself, to feel cheated, disappointed.

'Not this year. . . . Next April I should say. . . . You'll get the proofs around January . . .' Proofs of what? Did that mean the payment – proof positive that they were going to publish it or proof negative that they'd decided after all not to. . . . 'But they are going to . . . to take it?' 'Yes, yes. You'll get £25 right away – that is on signature and the other twenty-five on publishing day.' 'The proof?' 'Don't worry about those, I'll go through them with you if you like – or at any rate I'll give you a key to the ciphers – I think we've got one somewhere.'

Ciphers? What ciphers? Key? What sort of key? Would his manuscript be shut up in a box so that no one could steal it – was it as important as that? Would it be in a safe which had a special cipher which no burglar could open – and which he, Chris, would have access to – only he and Martin, and – possibly – Nightingale?

'Do come in, do come in . . . sit down won't you. I won't be a moment.' He made a show of looking through some papers, tapped his silver biro on his front teeth, and regarded Chris uncertainly. 'Well now . . . Yes, come in, Mrs Plaice.'

A plump, sad elderly woman, whose sticky hair showed signs of having been in curlers all night and not combed out, waddled towards the desk. She wore a green nylon overall, the sleeves turned up to above the folding-skin of her elbows. She placed a cup of tea in front of Martin? or Nightingale? slopping it over on to the petit-beurre biscuit that was balanced precariously on the saucer.

'Thank you, Mrs Plaice, you're a dear.' Mrs Plaice had gone out of the door and was about to shut it when he said, 'Oh, I'm sorry, would you like a cup of . . .' and half rose as if to call the tea-woman back.

'No thank you.'

'Sure? Are you certain?'

'Really not.'

'I can easily call her back.'

'No . . . really, I'm a coffee man myself.'

'I see.' Martin (or Nightingale) smiled and relaxed again. 'Well now,' he resumed, after a gulp of tea which was evidently cold because he gulped some more before going on . . . 'by the way, may I call you John?'

Chris hesitated, but saw no reason why he shouldn't comply.

'Of course,' he said, 'anything you like.'

'Fine. Fine. Well, John, the thing is – I must tell you frankly, we're a new firm, just beginning, in fact, and we're on the look-out for new, scintillating, if I may use the word, talent.'

He pressed a button. A woman's voice said what might have been 'Yes' from the machine on the desk. Martin-Nightingale seemed surprised it had answered, 'Oh,' he said, 'hallo, Miss er . . . can you bring me' – he looked up at Chris . . . 'what's the name of your book again?'

'Again?' said Chris.

'The title.'

'It hasn't got one . . .'

'Miss . . . er . . . have you got a typescript there without a title?' The machine said a longish sentence which sounded coarse.

'Oh, I see . . . yes, well . . . perhaps if you'd go through them – you might bring a sample few in. *Would* you? Oh, that's sweet of you.' Not that the voice had answered. He switched off the machine.

'Well now,' he said, 'we shall have to think of a title. Any ideas?' He rose from his desk and went towards the book-shelf.

'Not really,' said Chris, 'may I call you Martin?'

Nightingale turned round puzzled. 'Martin?' he said. 'I mean Nightingale,' said Chris. 'May I call you Nightingale?' I shan't call him Nightie till I know him better.

'Oh, good Lord, no,' said Martin. He looked delighted. 'Good Lord no. I see your point. Martin and Nightingale. No, no, John, I'm Peter.' He pulled a reference book out of the shelves. 'Here we are,' he said, 'Shakespeare. Frightfully good for titles. Let's try *Hamlet* for a start. Any idea what page "To be or not to be" is on?'

A young woman in forbidding glasses had come in with a pile of four or five manuscripts, and was plonking them in front of him.

'You'll recognise your own typing I expect,' she said to Chris – and turning gave him an unaffected smile. He sat up with surprise and pleasure.

'The one with the brown paper cover's mine,' he said.

There were two typed letters pinned on to the first page. Peter ignored him and read them to himself.

'Yes,' he said, 'I see. Well. Number one reader doesn't see much point in publishing it but he liked the end. Number two . . . Yes. Number two reader suggests you cut the ending, says you've used the same adjective twice on page 21, and you'll have to change the telephone number, it may be a listed one. Frankly, John, we're bound to lose money on any novel we publish. No one buys them. The printing costs have rocketed . . . have you any idea how much it costs to produce a book these days?'

He was leaning forward, serious, on familiar ground now.

'Why publish any then?'

It certainly sounded a mug's game, Chris was all on Peter's side.

'It's our policy . . . we like to encourage the young.'

Chris was amazed that such altruism should exist in the publishing world. These chaps were no better off than himself, how did they live?

'How can you survive?' he asked.

'That's the question,' said Peter, 'that is the question . . . to be or not to be . . . well we have to rely on school textbooks;

biographies; and porno of course, though good porno is rare. You don't write porno? No. Frankly, if you could, you could throw away this stuff, do yourself and us a favour. If you want my advice, John, go and live with a goat for a couple of years, and report your experiences. And hers. Nanny-goat of course. You'd make a fortune.'

The squiggle he now knew as Oscar or Oscar Townley lay at the bottom of the page. The first line, as his left hand easing down the page uncovered it, was of course Dean Street. Then, as his hand descended further, 'Dear Chris, . . . diddle, diddle . . . go and see the jacket design . . . diddle diddle . . . Squiggle'

This was life. This was how authors lived, they lay on their backs in bed, while their girl brought them coffee, and then they got up slowly, having received a letter from their agent, and took a taxi – well, the Tube perhaps, or a bus – to their publishers, and gave a nod of yea or nay to a specially designed cover of their forthcoming publication. As an old man he would tell his son and his grandson how he too had started from nothing before suddenly success overtook him, and he found himself famous overnight.

'Hallo! Nice to see you. What can I do for you?'

The euphoria dropped as quickly as a gush of water.

'I was told . . . I've come to see the jacket design.'

'The jacket . . . ?' Had he expected Chris to add 'potato'? 'Design.'

'Oh yes, of course, just a mo.' He pushed the button on the intercom. and was as surprised and delighted as he'd always been at the voice's response. 'Oh hallo! I say, can you ask publicity if they've got anything on . . . ? Er . . . yes, that's right, Mr er . . . oh good; jolly good-oh. Buzz them and tell them we'll be right over will you? I'll come with you,' he beamed at Chris.

They walked along the corridor and down some stairs and across another corridor. The door was open. 'May we come in?' he said ingratiatingly. A neat plump man with glasses shook Chris's hand.

'Hope you'll like it,' he said. 'We think it's smashing.'

Chris's spirits rose rapidly to fever-pitch. Why, he wondered, when he cared so little, should every friendly gesture and every unmeaningful slight have such an effect on the graph of his metabolism? They went to a desk where were strewn a number of drawings. 'This is the one we've chosen,' said the plump man, proudly. It was a tinted picture of a pretty young woman with a round face, and fair hair, holding in her hand what looked like a sheet of music.

'It's very nice,' Chris heard himself say, when he could bear his own silence no longer. 'But I don't think it's mine.'

'It's for your book, yes. Smashing, isn't it?'

'But my book's about a . . .'

'A child pianist, isn't it?'

'Well no, I mean yes – but he's a boy.'

'Oh, I see.' The plump man seemed a little less happy. Peter came to the rescue, 'Well, if we cut the hair a bit shorter, not too short, young men wear their hair nearly as long as this don't they, especially if they're artistically inclined. Ha, ha! I'm sure the artist won't mind.'

'Can't do that,' said the plump man.

'Why, isn't this a proof?'

'Yes, but if you want it out by the autumn he can't play around with it. He's got too much on his plate.'

'I see. Well . . .' he began to wax enthusiastic, 'now I look at it again, it could be a boy. Definitely.'

Chris said, 'But my boy's a moron.'

Both men laughed uncomfortably.

'The boy in my book,' said Chris, 'is *moronic*.'

'Well, you can't sell a book with an unattractive cover,' said the plump man.

'This will do very well, very well, *thank you*,' Peter said, and he led Chris by the elbow along the passage and up the stairs. 'These publicity boys really know what they're doing,' he explained on the way, 'they know the market. It's very difficult to sell a book at all, and unless you have a pretty face on a cover you're not likely to go far.'

'But the artist must have known,' Chris felt ludicrously near to weeping like a child. . . .

'Well, a young pianist . . . could be either sex, couldn't it? I expect he was just told "a young pianist". Personally I'm jolly pleased with it, I think it *looks* like a boy.'

'But if you can only sell a book with a pretty *girl* on the cover . . .'

'We'll sell it, we'll sell it . . . ah, here's Mrs P with a cuppa. Thank you so very much Mrs P . . . can't I tempt you to some tea?'

He was pretending that it didn't matter, rehearsing failure in order to exorcise it, though in truth he now cared very much less than he would have thought it possible a year ago. A tiny ember of hope, success-fantasy, was being fanned by the thought that tomorrow, Monday, the book would be out. He might see it displayed in a shop. What did it matter if it had a fatuous cover, if fatuous covers were what sold books? He might read a review of it . . . innumerable half-formulated thoughts passed through his brain and conveyed themselves to his senses, which surprised him by still being able to quiver.

They were sitting at 'supper'. Not that he cared now about his parents' social behaviour, or what they called anything. Claire didn't notice, not only because she came from the same sort of background, but because she noticed things and people only with her feelings, never with her judgement. His parents were wary he noticed of treading on anything that might prove to be one of his corns. They didn't mention how long it was since he had visited them, didn't ask if he was working, or about his money affairs. They chatted as if to acquaintances of short-standing . . . and he was beginning to feel slighted that perhaps after all they didn't really care about anything he did, had outgrown him as he had them, when his mother unexpectedly said, 'I've ordered a copy, but they wanted to know the name of the publishers.' This was obviously a question, but he preferred to think it was a statement, and didn't reply. To his amazement his father added, 'Two. You've ordered two copies. One for me.'

He felt a terrible blush over his whole body, at the same time wishing they wouldn't read it (but how could he stop them?) and visualising his sales going up by dozens as different booksellers passed on the message: 'We've been asked for a couple of copies already – who are the publishers?'

He spent the evening convinced that his parents were two-dimensional, that no one had breathed reality into them, that they had been cut out of a paper pattern whose model was itself an uninspired piece of work. The people he had lost, whom he had once lived with for a year, but whose existence he no longer believed in, nor wanted to think about, were nevertheless, when he had known them, more vivid, more individually alive than the people who were responsible for his own existence. He felt alienated, and desperately lonely. The only way to believe in someone, he thought, as he looked objectively at the three people sitting at table with him, was to invent them. They might get out of hand, but they would at the same time surprise him and feel a part of him.

Claire had been out and bought the papers; even early editions of the Evenings. She had also brought him a long-stalked dark red rose with unwelcome hard thorns, and the letter she had picked up from the hall.

'Happy day,' she said, and added her usual, 'I'll make coffee.'

He saw the rose as a bad omen, silly bitch why did she want to spoil his chances by giving him an ill-luck token? He had a desire to crush it, but got up instead and laid it on the window-sill out of his reach. Why had she bought the papers? Did she think reviews came out the day that books were published? Any fool knew (he himself had found out about six months' previously) that certain papers had their book reviews on certain days, and there'd be nothing in any of them, except perhaps *The Financial Times*, today. She'd even gone to the expense of buying the *Mirror* and the *Express*, though any fool knew that these never carried book reviews at all. Or very seldom.

He opened two quickly just in case and then threw them on the floor. He didn't feel like opening the others – he'd wait till Sunday and then go out by himself on some pretext and get the lot and sit in the park and look at them. He opened the letter. The writing was neat; maybe his first fan?

Dear Chris,

Your mother is naturally very excited about the 'forthcoming event!' We both wish you the very greatest success and you may be sure we shall be studying the National Papers to see what they say of you.

Our news is very much the same as usual; we are not very adventurous in our old age, though your mother likes to follow the plays on television and I still take an interest in the sporting events.

I hope this venture brings you prosperity; I remain,

Your affectionate father.

(He had nearly written 'servant'). It was obvious that he'd posted it before he had seen Chris the day before – probably 'edited' it earlier in the week, copying it out from a rough.

Middle-age descended on Chris suddenly, without warning,

as the letter pushed his parents into an elderly and speedy descent. He saw himself just before the brow of his own peak – and shut his eyes with horror as he recognised it to be a mound, no higher than a tuft for a cemetery headstone.

He wanted to go out alone, to walk into bookshops alone, and not to be shamed in front of anyone; Claire would understand, wouldn't think a whit less of him for failure, yet he didn't want her. He was totally, and wished to be totally, alone. And yet his own meanness was so nauseating to him that when she brought the coffee, he said, 'Shall we go round the bookshops, and see . . . ?'

She said, 'I must work this morning – I'll meet you somewhere this afternoon; I've got . . .'

She put her head down to cover the unaccustomed lie.

He accepted the game; knew how difficult it was for her to play, and in an excess of genuine warmth put his arm round her shoulders. The coffee-pot lurched, spilt much of its contents on to the sheet. Unless Chris trod carefully, lyingly, this sort of mishap always occurred. 'I was never meant to be sincere,' he thought.

He planned to leave Dillon's and Truslove and Hanson till the afternoon, when she would be with him; and to tackle himself in the morning six others. He'd start off at Selfridges then go on to John Menzies in the Strand, and Better Books and Foyles in Charing Cross Road. He would buy one copy from each shop, just to get the ball rolling – and, just in case one of them hadn't got it on display, he prepared himself by snubbing himself in advance in various male and female voices. 'What title?' 'Who's the publisher?' 'Sorry, no.' And his reply would be gracious, smiling, 'Pity, I've heard it's very good,' or 'Oh, I was recommended it,' in a surprised, baffled voice.

As it was, he saw no copy in any of the shops, and hadn't the courage either to ask an assistant if they had it, or to order it.

182

He had trouble getting rid of Claire. She made excuses, followed him when he found a cheaper room, certain in her femininity that he needed her, and was trying to get rid of her for her own sake. She even stopped concentrating on her work, and paid her whole day's attention to him.

Eventually his need to be alone was so great that he destroyed her cruelly with words from which he hoped at the time she would never recover. She went then. He disdained drugs and drink not only because they cost money, but because they did not suit his purpose. He wanted to be unaccommodated man, though even here he knew he was cheating, because he found some sort of accommodation in the most sordid room he could that did not entail sleeping with others. He set out a pattern for himself of the barest necessities of being alive. Between queuing for National Assistance and being sent for interviews for prospective jobs (none of which were successful of course because he saw to it that he made the worst possible impression) he watched a bowl of milk and a hunk of bread which he had placed carefully by his bed, take their different paths through colour and texture to their own private disintegrations. He was fascinated. His eyes were held for hours by the bowl of milk which he fancied changed as he watched.

His own disintegration was noticeable, neither to himself nor anyone else. His hair would grow no longer than to his shoulders, his beard though pleasingly straggly attained no more than an inch in length, the dirt he accumulated through an aversion to water was no more than a greying of the skin; only the smell of him stood out from the crowd.

Ten months passed, and then an unpredictable and extraordinary thing happened. He saw a letter with his name lying on the stone floor downstairs. It had been re-addressed from his parents' home in the neat hand of his father; but it had evidently not been opened.

The sight of it panicked him at the same time as he felt a ray dart through his chest and clutch at the valves of his heart. Slowly he went back up the stairs and fetched some coins. He would breakfast.

He would go to a café and order coffee and a roll. The thought of it set his saliva running. He became aware of other parts of his body; he could feel his mind ticking over, caught his ears catching the sound of traffic. He bent down to pick up the envelope. It had an Australian stamp and postmark. He suspected a hoax. He put it quickly, surreptitiously, into his pocket and aware of the motions his legs made in walking he opened the front door and started along the pavement.

He would choose. Choose where to breakfast. There were three cafés he knew of – one of which he had been into two or three times when he'd first moved here. It was frequented by seedy individuals like himself, but most of them old, in threadbare coats, the pockets unstitched, limply hanging. Seedy. What a strange word . . . it didn't mean to the bare essentials, to the seed; what could that -y signify when juxtaposed with seed? Needy meant *in* need – beefy *of* beef, streaky *with* streaks, pithy full of pith, but what by, with, from, of, or in, seed could apply to the unwell, uncared for types like himself, he wondered. He recognised that he needed this word game he was playing to keep himself moving along the pavement without concentrating too unbearably on the tantalising envelope in his pocket.

He passed by café No. 1, putting off the actual drinking of hot coffee and eating of bread and opening of the letter, as a prisoner of war will put off opening a Red Cross food parcel, making the most of it, taking the longest over it, arranging his bed for it, allowing the juices to accumulate for it. Once opened the desire would become a mite less intense; once tasted the drop in anticipation was sheer, once eaten there was nothing left but regret and the long, long wait for another parcel.

His heart held still then thumped heavily before he had the sense to step out of her path and into a doorway – but surely she would not anyway have recognised him? Along the pavement was coming a young woman with greasy hair, in an old grey cloak, pushing a pram. Of course, of course, these creations which were none of his, reproduced themselves without any help from their maker. If he, Chris, wanted a newborn member of his book, he'd have to think him up. Not so the Almighty. He'd arranged things in such a lazy fashion, that his creatures did it for themselves; he simply let loose a few, and let them get on with it. In the pram, his mind had time to visualise, would be a tiny Claire replica in a tiny cloak, with tiny unstockinged dirty legs and teeny black toe-nails. Or perhaps not. Marriage was apt to turn the offspring of the petty bourgeoisie, however in their youthful days they rejected the idea, into bourgeois mums and dads. In the pram he guessed, would more likely be a scrubbed one-year-old, in a persil-white coat, surrounded by the morning's shopping of cornflakes, milk and orange-juice.

The pram and its pusher passed him now where he had turned up a step and backed against a glass shop-door; and he saw that it was not Claire after all, but only one of the thousands like her; that the cloak was not grey, but a dull brown, and that in the pram were the cornflakes clearly visible on the top of a carrier-bag – but no baby.

He stepped back onto the pavement, and, his back to the receding back, he continued on his way.

He shuffled into café No. 2 having seen through the open door an empty table. It was slopped with tea and the remains of another customer's meal, but he quickened his pace to appropriate it, as he saw that a man was at the counter. The man, having ordered before him, would naturally turn round and take the empty table. Chris decided to feign ignorance of having to go up to the counter – then changed his mind and decided to sip from the used cup as if he'd been there for some time; changed his mind again because, of course, the man at the counter would have noticed there was no one there when he came in, and decided to wave at a non-existent pal passing in the street just as the man turned. The man hesitated, but was obviously not an aggressor, and disappointed, sat himself and his egg and chips at another tea-spilt table, occupied by three other men.

Chris got up warily, leaned, his fingertips still touching his appropriated table, and said meekly, 'Cup of coffee please and a cheese roll.' The very word cheese started his saliva ducts dribbling again. He sat down and up again as the roll and coffee were plonked on the counter. 'Twelve,' she said. He took a grateful gulp of coffee, felt the blood warm downwards to one foot, and, strangely, up from the other, until he was suffused with passable comfort. One bite, and then the letter. Then, if the letter were a hoax, or worse, there was a whole cup of coffee and a whole roll to comfort himself with before restarting his non-existence. He studied the envelope, gleaning no further clue from it. With his heart throbbing as if a 100-mile-an-hour train were descending upon him, he opened it. There was a sheet and a half (or should it be there *were* . . . did the half count as a 'were' being more than one, or a 'was' being less than two, he wondered) of writing on narrow lined paper. But there was also, and this was the climactic jump, an enclosure: a cutting of newsprint.

There would still be pleasure, or rather the putting off of catastrophe, in delay, even if he gave himself the pleasure, or the pain, of reading the letter. He looked first at the signature (the writer had covered the front and back of the first sheet, and the front of the second). Dorothy Paring. The writing was elderly, that is, it was like his mother's rounded, small, undeveloped since it had been taught at school how to form letters. He turned to the start and, without noticing, took another gulp of the warm coffee:

Dear Chris,

I hope you don't mind if I call you that, although you won't remember me but I used to call on your mother when you were a little boy. I haven't heard from her for the last two or three years, and I've always been meaning to write but somehow it gets put off. I'm supposing you are still at the same address as I have in my book. I came out here to visit my son and daughter-in-law many years ago, and I quite took to the place, so I stayed on.

I was delighted to read in the newspaper that you had written a book. That is to say, I think it must be the little Chris I knew, but if it's another writer of the same name please forgive me. I am enclosing the review. I'm quite proud to have met a real writer. I always thought you'd do well. My fondest regards to you and your mother and your father, though I don't suppose he'll remember me.

Yours sincerely,
Dorothy Paring

Well! It was a fan letter! Little matter that she hadn't read the book, she was a fan all right and proud to know him. She'd always known he would . . . how had she put it? . . . he re-read the letter, slowly now, savouring it; took time off between pages to eat and drink. He couldn't remember when he'd felt so alive. And there was still the bonus in store for him. A notice. Someone, somewhere, had actually noticed his book. To hell with England; he'd emigrate. Australia was obviously where all the happening was. A man could write in a country like that; begin a new life. He hesitated whether to go back to his room before reading the cutting, or stay here in the warmth of the café with its encouraging atmosphere of slopped tea and seedy men.

He decided to stay. He finished his meal, slowly drawing up the last crumbs on to a licked finger, leaned back, and unfolded the long thin cutting.

Mrs Paring had stuck the page heading on to the top paragraph: *Melbourne Press*. So far so good. *Melbourne Press* sounded impressive, and she was perceptive enough to realise that he'd want to know in which newspaper his notice had been printed. As, however, the heading was stuck on to the middle of a paragraph, the first line or two made little sense, but were evidently not about *his* book as the characters mentioned were not his, and included a sheep-dog. The paragraph finished near the bottom of the page (the other side of the cutting, he quickly ascertained, was part of a photograph, possibly an advertisement). Near the bottom as he turned back to read again was another heading BITS AND PIECES. And lo and behold and behold and lo, and hold and below, and blow me if and low low breathe and blow, there was the title of his book, and, yes, his name! His *name*! In print!

His wasn't the only notice below BITS AND PIECES; there was another title and name below his, but between the two was the comment 'Readable.' Just the one word: 'Readable.' Well, anyway, his name was above the other fellow's, and it was a good notice too. 'Readable' meant it was readable, not only able to be read, but happily able to be read. The fellow had enjoyed it. The fellow had perception. Who was he? What was he like? The bottom of the page was signed D.B. That meant the fellow had read *all* the books that were written on this page, that meant that he had experience, a professional attitude towards reading books, and in his considered opinion Chris's book was readable. He'd write him a letter: 'Dear D.B. Many thanks for your . . .' No. 'Dear D.B., I read with interest your assessment . . .' or perhaps, 'Dear D.B. Please may I have your autograph?'

The coffee, the letter, the cutting stirred in Chris a sensation he had not had since the day he had gone into Hyde Park to write. The sensation was powerful. He opened his nostrils to it; it was the trembling, necessitous, daring, stirring of desire. The desire to buy paper and pencil and write a book.